POACHING SPREE

WASHINGTON FISH & WILDLIFE DETECTIVE TODD A. VANDIVERT (RETIRED)

Printed by: **Create Space**
Distributed by: **www.amazon.com**

ISBN- **978-1-7048-26875**

THIS BOOK IS FICTION. The names, characters, locations, and events are either the products of the author's imagination or used in a fictitious manner. Any resemblance to actual persons, living or dead, or actual events is purely coincidental.

Cover created by- **Bruce Weild, www.b-creative.ca/design**

DEDICATION

To the courageous women and men who put their lives on the line to preserve and protect our great natural resources;

thank you.

"ETHICAL BEHAVIOR IS DOING THE RIGHT THING WHEN NO ONE ELSE IS WATCHING- EVEN WHEN DOING THE WRONG THING IS LEGAL."

— ALDO LEOPOLD –

WRITTEN BY: TODD A. VANDIVERT

WILDLIFE JUSTICE SERIES

(FICTION)

POACHING SPREE

TO PROTECT A PREDATOR

A FALCON'S TALE

LETHAL REMOVAL

DEEP TROUBLE

FOR YOUR PROTECTION

HUNTING THE HUNTERS

FOLLOW THE WATER

POACHER'S PEAK

NON-FICTION

OPERATION CODY

GAME WARDENS AND POACHERS

CHAPTER 1

With his arm hair matted down in dark sticky blood and his somewhat clean uniform shirt hanging from the limb of a nearby ponderosa pine, Game Warden Clayton Newberry continued his search for the poacher's bullet. The Vicks VapoRub, smeared on his upper lip, helped mask the horrific smell enough for Clay to cut through the rotting tissue without puking. A metal detector had provided him with a general idea of where the bullet was, but getting his hands on it was proving to be more difficult.

Recovering the bullet from the mule deer buck's carcass was the last step Clay would take in processing this poaching scene. He had already taken nineteen crime scene photos, collected DNA samples from the dead buck, photographed the boot prints left around the carcass, and marked the exact location on his GPS. Had the carcass been fresh, Clay would also have recorded the internal temperature of the deer and the ambient air temperature in an effort to determine a rough time of death. These tasks had become far too routine to Clay in recent months.

Immediately upon arrival at the scene, Clay had walked the logging road above the kill site to identify all locations from which the fatal shot may have been fired. Knowing most poachers fire from inside a vehicle or at least adjacent to one, Clay dragged his boot heel to mark the two opposite ends of a 30-yard stretch of road. This small window in the roadside vegetation would have provided the only opening from which the poached animal would have been visible from the road. Clay then used his rangefinder to measure the distance-178 yards. It was a shot almost anyone could easily make with a scoped rifle.

USFS (United States Forest Service) Road 2310 is a dead-end road that peels off the 23 Mainline. The USFS 23 Mainline originates from the Wright Road—a county road that then leads into the small town of Oroville, WA, in Okanogan County. If one were driving up the 2310 Road, the poached buck would be found lying down a steep hill off the left side of the road. This meant the person who poached this particular buck most likely fired either from the driver's side window or had exited the truck and fired from the left side of the vehicle. Either way, if they shot a right-handed rifle and had ejected a spent shell casing, it would have landed either back in the truck or on the left side of this 30-yard stretch of gravel road. But 40 minutes of searching with a metal detector produced no shell casings. Nothing. Just like with the other poaching incidents, this scene provided virtually zero evidence of value in locating a suspect.

With the sting of sweat dribbling into his eyes, Newberry muttered to himself as he slowly rolled the flattened bullet between his bloody fingers. "Thirty-three! This makes thirty-friggin'-three." He already knew the bullet he had found lodged between the buck's ribcage and hide was far too damaged to provide reliable forensics evidence.

The single bullet had entered the buck from high and left on the buck's body cavity. The bullet had begun to expand (mushroom) as it penetrated the hide, even before slamming into the left front shoulder blade at nearly 3,000 feet per second, instantly splintering the formattable bone. What came through the disintegrated shoulder was a

6

badly mashed lead projectile along with several minute particles of lead and shards of the copper alloy bullet jacket. The bullet, in its fragmented state, had then traveled through the buck's left lung, heart, right lung, and finally the ribs before running out of energy and coming to rest just under the hide of the recently deceased deer. Unfortunately for Clay, the rifling impressions left on the bullet as it was fired were fragmented along with the bullet's copper jacket.

Unlike their city and county law enforcement counterparts, game wardens are their own CSI teams. Through training and experience, wardens across North America make up some of the best overall cops on Earth. Wardens routinely work cases from the initial report through the evidence collection/processing, interrogation, and arrest—all without assistance. Only when a case arrives at the point of prosecution does the warden need outside help, and this happens to be the area in which most poaching cases fall short. Prosecutors frequently consider poaching to be a "victimless" crime, and thus they shove it far down on their priority list, often resolving egregious poaching cases with a mere hand slap. But this does not happen with thirty-three bodies.

Whoever was responsible for this poaching spree was going to pay. In Clay's thirty-plus years as a warden, he had handled only about twelve big game animals (deer, elk, moose, and bear), which had been shot and intentionally left to rot. Of those twelve cases, Clay had arrested and convicted the poachers on all but four, and those four remained open cases.

In just the last year, Clay had at least thirty-three big game animals poached right out from under his nose. Each animal had been shot in easily accessible areas and on public lands; however, this deer was the first kill visible from a public road. Clay wasn't naive enough to think the thirty-three kill scenes were the only ones out there in his patrol area. These thirty-three were simply the ones he had found or had been turned in by citizens. He guessed he probably had only identified a small fraction of the animals slaughtered by these spree killers, yet he didn't have a clue who was responsible.

As he steered his patrol truck back home, Clay wondered just what the hell was going on. Was all of this some kind of twisted payback from someone he has arrested in the past? Were these the acts of a group of demented drug-fueled teenagers? Who would do this and why? Even the hard-core poachers he had dealt with in the past took something from the animals: the head, the antlers, the meat, something.

The first such incident in this long string of kills was back in September of last year when a grouse hunter, attracted by a noisy gathering of crows, found the carcasses of three dead black bears. The bears, a sow, and two cubs had each been shot and left to rot. By the time the grouse hunter had found the carcasses, they had been ravaged by a multitude of scavengers, from coyotes to insects, until there was little left but a pile of hair and bones—bones with bullet holes. As far as Clay could tell, nothing had been removed from any of the three bears. The claws, teeth, hide, and skulls of a bear are the most commonly retained "trophy" parts; yet all were intact on these bears.

Now, eleven months and thirty-three poached animals later, Clay was no closer to solving these cases. He had gathered a ton of physical evidence—all of which had proven to be worthless in locating suspects. Clay had recovered twenty-one bullets from eighteen of the

8

thirty-three animals poached. He had footprint impressions, tire track impressions, crime scene photos, measurements, and animal DNA, but he had nothing which would lead to the responsible individual or individuals. Not one fingerprint. Not one cigarette butt with human DNA. Not a single trail camera photo. Nothing.

Clay knew the physical evidence he currently had would go a long way toward convicting the suspect or suspects once identified, but until that time, it was just taking up space.

CHAPTER 2

Her hands shook as Cricket carefully opened the foil and cellophane encased 8-ball (an eighth of an ounce or 3.5 grams) of "brown." Cricket, so named because she is small, loud, and obnoxious, hovered over the eighth of an ounce, guarding it with her life. This 8-ball was worth far more than the $300 it would cost on the street, as Cricket was looking forward to the stronger and longer-lasting high offered by the brown heroin over her regular black tar.

Twenty-year-old Jessica "Cricket" Tiller and her boyfriend Blake occupied one of the three bedrooms in the thirty-one-year-old single-wide, which they shared with three others. The trailer rested on a forty-foot-wide strip of ground in the Riverside Mobile Home Park. Currently home alone, she was feverishly working to stave off withdrawals by feeding her body the heroin it needed to survive, hopefully before the roommates arrived home.

A user since fifteen years of age, Cricket had the process down to a science. After separating out a chunk of heroin about the size of a couple of Tic-Tacs, she brought out her hype kit, consisting of a bent and blackened spoon, five syringes (with capped needles), a lighter, a candle, and a bunch of small cotton balls. Cricket carefully loaded the spoon with the brown, and then using the syringe, she added water to the spoon. Once the candle had heated the mixture to the boiling point, it was almost ready. Next, a small cotton ball was rolled tightly between her filthy fingers until it was ready to be dropped into the center of the spoon. Instantly, the cotton absorbed the liquefied heroin, allowing Cricket to filter the liquid as it was drawn up from the spoon.

10

With the syringe loaded, Cricket was both nervous and excited to try the brown.

Like so many others in the U.S., Jessica had become addicted to opioids after using Oxycontin as a boost when partying with high school friends. What started as an occasional party aid soon became a full-blown addiction. Cricket's hometown of Omak, Washington, seemed to have quite an appetite for heroin, with heroin sales far overtaking meth in recent years even though the local price of meth had recently dropped significantly. Oxy was getting harder to find and more expensive, so many opioid users were forced to switch to heroin to feed their addictions. The Okanogan Valley is made up of several small rural towns, some with high drug addiction rates.

The valley's heroin supply normally came from Mexico, through California, to Seattle. From Seattle, the loads were broken down further and sent to virtually each and every town in the state of Washington. Running the dope from Mexico north to Seattle was left to Mexican cartel members, but the smaller loads were handled by a wide variety of mid-level drug traffickers. Until a few months back, at least 90% of the heroin in the Okanogan Valley was black tar from Mexico, but within the last couple of years, police began finding brown heroin on many users.

Heroin comes in all shades but is normally broken down into three categories: black tar, brown, or white (also called China White). Black tar, named such because of its sticky tar-like appearance, is the garbage of the heroin world. Born in Mexico, black tar is poorly refined and has low potency, yet black tar is the cheapest and most readily available heroin in the western U.S.

11

Originating in Southeast Asia and Afghanistan, China White is almost unheard of in Washington. It is both very expensive and very potent.

Brown heroin is middle-class heroin—not too cheap and not too expensive. Brown can have an extremely high potency/purity level or can be degraded by cutting agents, but when it's combined with fentanyl, it can easily become lethal. Often brought to the Pacific Northwest by way of Mexico, brown heroin most often originates in Southwest Asia.

A synthetic opioid, fentanyl can be up to 50 times more powerful than heroin. Produced in both China and Mexico (as well as some in North America), fentanyl is far cheaper per dose than heroin, but its reputation for delivering death scares many potential users into sticking with the heroin they are accustomed to. Being the kind, caring humans they are, drug dealers have come up with a way to maximize profits while providing their "customers" the product they so desire. An efficient dealer will turn one ounce of pure brown heroin into three by simply "cutting" the product with a mixture of baking soda and sucrose. Cutting dope is much like watering down alcohol; you simply produce more of a weaker product. Now that the dealer has tripled the volume of heroin, he has also created heroin that is a third of the potency of the uncut version, which will not bring back repeat customers. But by adding just a touch of fentanyl to the mix, the dealer has three full ounces of brown H, which is even more powerful than the original product. Everyone is happy.

It was just after three p.m. when Blake turned his 1993 Nissan pickup into the Riverside Mobile Home Park. After a hard day of

12

work, Blake couldn't wait to slam a shot and chill for the rest of the day. He worked his ass off and deserved a break. Blake was only a "recreational user" of heroin and could certainly give it up anytime he wanted to. He just didn't want to.

As Blake pulled his truck up to the rotting wooden steps at the trailer's front door, he noticed Cricket's car was the only car there. Perfect. It would just be him and Cricket getting high off the brown. He was getting sick and tired of the assholes they lived with and didn't trust them any further than he could throw them. Once he saved up some money, they would get their own place, get married, and then get clean. Blake really loved Cricket and was determined to make a better life for her—soon.

At a hair over five feet tall and 115 pounds, Jessica was always popular with the boys, making her a favorite of the party scene. As a high school freshman, Jessica was placed in the AP (Advanced Placement) classes, where she excelled in math and science. Jessica's teachers all hoped she would be able to break away from the horrible life she had at home and not follow the paths of her brothers (one of whom was still in the Walla Walla State Penitentiary), but they also knew the odds were stacked against her.

Well-known to local law enforcement, Cricket's stepfather was twice arrested for domestic violence against her mother but never convicted. An unemployed heavy equipment operator, Daryl spent the majority of his days getting high and bitching about everything from the old lady to the local cops. Only two things seemed to make Daryl happy: a taste of meth and the touch of Cricket's soft skin, but it had been a long time since Daryl had even seen the little princess. Ever

13

since she started hanging around that loser Blake, he had turned her against him. Someday, Daryl was going to run into that little prick out in the woods, and then he would give him what he deserved. You can hide a lot of bodies in the hills.

Blake could hear Cricket's stupid *House Hunter's* show through the front door as he climbed the three wooden steps. After finding nothing in the living room, Blake headed to the back bedroom—their bedroom.

It's not like you see on TV. Cricket wasn't flopped over the bed with a needle hanging from her arm as it dangled off the side. At first, Blake thought she was just screwing around with him because she looked perfectly normal lying in bed and staring at the ceiling. As a matter of fact, Cricket had never looked so peaceful and pretty. With her blonde hair pulled back into a ponytail and resting on a pillow, she could have just been asleep, but Blake knew better; he had seen this before. He felt for a pulse. There was none. Shaking her didn't do the trick, nor did screaming in her face arouse her. She was gone.

"Focus. Fucking focus!" Blake muttered through his tears. He had to think. There was nothing he could do for Cricket; she was gone. It was time to look out for number one. First things first. He had to get rid of the dope. Blake searched through the trailer's closets until he found an empty cardboard box, which he instantly filled with the drugs and drug paraphernalia he and Cricket shared together. Next came the guns—the loaded Mossberg .30-06 rifle behind the seat of his pickup, the Ruger 10/22 .22 rifle in the bedroom closet, and the loaded H&R single shot 12 gauge under the bed. Finally, he dealt with the ammunition and knives that went with the guns. These were wrapped

14

in a blanket, held in a tight wrap with duct tape, and placed near the front door.

Blake didn't have access to the entire trailer, as his "room-mates" had locked their own bedrooms, but he had completed removing anything he thought would be of interest to the police. He momentarily thought about leaving his roomies a note telling them they might want to prepare for a police visit, but he thought better of it. A phone call would be better.

After loading the items into his truck, there was only one task left. For that task, Blake brought in a well-used, blue plastic tarp from his truck. Blake wasn't stupid. He knew the cops would be looking for anyone associated with Cricket's death, and he sure as shit didn't need that kind of attention, not with his new job and all, so he scoured their bedroom for gloves. When Blake realized no gloves were to be found, he donned a pair of socks over his hands. After spreading the tarp out on the bedroom floor, Blake gently picked Cricket off the bed and placed her in the center of the filthy tarp.

Puke welled up in Blake's throat as he sat and stared at her. She was the only real girlfriend he ever had and the only person he gave a shit about at all. Now she was gone, and he was fucked if he didn't get rid of her body. Looking down at his shaking hands as he began to wrap the tarp around her body, he chuckled. In his sock gloves, Blake's hands looked like two sock-puppets. Two stupid hand-puppets were wrapping his soulmate in a tarp and duct tape. He couldn't believe it. This shit was insane. As soon as he found a place for Cricket, he was gonna slam the same load that Cricket had. He should

15

have been there with her. It should have been him and would have been if she had waited.

Clear Creek Road seemed like the perfect spot. No houses and very little traffic meant no chance of ending up on someone's home security camera. After turning off Hwy. 97, Blake continued up Clear Creek about eight miles before reaching a large flat area commonly used for hunters' camps. Since the hunting season was not open for another couple of months, all was quiet. Blake was sure someone would find Jessica wrapped in a tarp lying out in the open flat within 24 hours, but if he didn't hear about it on the news, he would call in anonymously in a couple of days.

Now he just had to get over to Devon's place to stash his shit until things calmed down.

CHAPTER 3

A lot of things about rifle ballistics are weird. For example, a .308 rifle fires a bullet that is .308" in diameter, but a .270 rifle fires a bullet that is .277" in diameter, which is a lot closer to .280 than .270. But the .280 rifle fires a .284" diameter bullet. Then there's the hugely popular .30-06, so named because it fires a .30 caliber bullet (which actually has a .308" diameter), and the cartridge was designed in 1906—hence the .30-06. The lever-action 30-30 again uses the .30 (.308) caliber bullet and originally used 30 grains of smokeless powder, and so on.

It always drives Clay nuts when someone refers to rifle cartridges as "bullets" or "shells." Bullets were simply one of the four components of a cartridge; the case or casing (normally brass), the bullet (normally lead surrounded in a copper alloy jacket), the powder, and the primer (which creates the ignition spark when struck by the firing pin). Since the Chinese invented firearms around a thousand years ago, they haven't changed all that much. A lead projectile is sent hurling down a cylindrical barrel by the gases created by a charge of gunpowder, which had been ignited by a spark. Modern firearms are faster, more powerful, more accurate, and far more reliable than those first Chinese weapons, but they are still strikingly similar in many ways.

One great advancement in firearms design was the addition of rifling to the barrels of rifles and pistols (very few shotgun barrels are rifled). Rifling is a process by which helical grooves are machined into the inner surface of the firearm's barrel. The barrel "lands" are the

17

uncut surface of the inner barrel, which protrudes furthest toward the center of the barrel. The barrel "grooves" are the channels machined into the barrel surface. The purpose of these lands and grooves is to spin the bullet as it travels down the barrel. After the bullet leaves the barrel muzzle (the terminal end of a barrel), it will continue to spin, thus increasing the bullet's stability and accuracy.

A rifled barrel will always have an equal number of lands and grooves, but the width, spacing, the number of these lands and grooves, twist rate, and the direction of the spin (whether the bullet has a right or left-handed spin) will vary from firearm to firearm.

Clay sat at his generous 8' wide reloading bench, which also served as his own personal ballistics forensics station. From his shirt breast pocket, he removed the pancaked bullet he had recovered from the poached deer he processed this morning. Dumping the bullet fragments from the unsealed evidence bag, he again realized how little value this would have to his case—that is, if he ever had a suspect.

Clay first submerged the bullet pieces into a solution of warm, soapy water. With a soft dental brush, he lightly brushed the blood and tissues off each bullet piece. After lightly patting the bullet dry and finishing the drying with Karen's hairdryer, he weighed all the bullet fragments together—163 grains. The grain is a measurement of the equivalent single grain of barley and is most commonly used in measuring the weight of ammunition components and arrows/broadheads.

The next step for Clay would normally be to determine the bullet diameter (which with a chart will provide the bullet caliber), the

18

number of lands and grooves, the twist of the barrel, and the width of the lands and grooves. With this particular bullet, Clay believed he was holding a .30 caliber (.308") bullet but couldn't be certain because of its horrible condition.

If a bullet recovered from a carcass/body is properly cleaned, that bullet will obviously never weigh more after being fired than before. Therefore, 163 grains of bullet fragments most likely had come from the largest of common .30 caliber projectiles—the 180-grain bullet. It is not uncommon for a bullet to lose some of its weight between the time the bullet was fired until it has been cleaned and weighed; in this case, the fragmented bullet had lost only 9.6% of its weight.

As a bullet travels down the barrel, the lands (the uncut or raised inside surface of the barrel) cut land impressions, which appear as grooves into the bullet as the barrel coaxes the bullet into a spin. During this process, the bullet loses a slight amount of mass and energy. When the bullet leaves the muzzle, it bears its own land and groove impressions. The lands are counted, the twist is determined (right or left), and by use of a caliper (tool to make precise measurements), the land and groove widths are measured. These characteristics are referred to as "class characteristics" because they are common among all firearms of that same barrel. For example, all 24" Ruger M77 Mark IV .308 rifles made in 1995 will have the exact same class characteristics.

On the other hand, there are individual characteristics unique to each individual firearm. These are the unique scratches, nicks, and imperfections in the barrel and actions of every firearm. Like fingerprints, the individual characteristics of a firearm will identify the

19

one individual firearm which fired a particular projectile. Clay felt quite comfortable working with class characteristics, but in no way was he capable of determining individual characteristics. That was state patrol crime lab stuff. Electron microscopes and such are used there, but it takes time (sometimes up to six months or longer) to get the results back. None of that was applicable to this particular bullet since it was just another smashed to hell .30 caliber bullet. Clay returned the bullet pieces to the evidence bag and sealed and labeled the bag. He reached into his gun safe, brought out a padded shipping envelope labeled "Poaching Spree," and added the bullet to the other twenty.

After wiping down his reloading bench, Clay sauntered into his living room. He grabbed his department-issued laptop from the counter and plopped into his overstuffed Costco recliner, affectionately named "The Command Center" by his wife, Karen.

A lot had changed in Clay's thirty years with Fish and Wildlife, but one of the biggest changes was in the officers they hire. Way back when game wardens were all rough around the edges, tough, hard-working men (when Clay was hired, the department was 100% male). In the good old days, technology played no role in the job at all. Arrests were made as the result of long, hard hours of work and determination. Hundreds of hours of surveillance, thousands of miles of patrol, and, most importantly, strong relationships with the local residents and law enforcement were the norm for every effective game warden. Contrary to what the general public believes, very few big game cases are made in the field as a result of a game warden discovering the crimes during routine patrol. In reality, cases are mostly made by information provided to the warden by citizens.

Game wardens invented community policing decades before mainstream law enforcement embraced it. In small communities, everyone knew the game warden, and everyone had an opinion of him or her—good or bad. Wardens who treated everyone, including violators, with respect and courtesy had much easier careers than those who treated everyone as the enemy. Clay's thirty-one-year-old sergeant was one of those people who never seemed to get it.

Sgt. Sean Dresken had promoted to sergeant just a few short years after being first hired as a "fish and wildlife officer" (Clay reserved the title of "Game Warden" to those who he felt truly deserved the respect that title deserved) and took the open sergeant position in Omak. Sergeant Sean was a young, arrogant ladder climber who had virtually no knowledge of game warden work. But for some reason, Sean left Clay pretty much alone. The young sergeant was in charge of the greatly understaffed Okanogan County detachment and its three officers: Clay, Lisa Bennington, and Joe Ramirez. Ramirez was still in training and would be for weeks to come, so the only other full-fledged fish and wildlife officer in the geographically largest county in the state was Lisa, who lived near Tonasket. With only two active officers to supervise, Dresken should have had plenty of time to assist his officers in the field, but for one reason or the other, he was always unavailable. He seemed to either be "in meetings" or conducting "administrative duties" at his small office in Omak.

Because the "Boy Wonder" was so obsessed with his image and what his superiors thought of him, he was always chasing stats. He was constantly saying "we" need more contacts (with the public), more citations, or more arrests, and he wanted big cases closed quickly.

21

Clay always believed stats never told the whole picture. To a large degree, it came down to the choice of quality vs. quantity, and Clay had always believed quality cases meant a hell of a lot more than a bunch of small, chippy tickets.

As he opened his department email account, Clay was instantly pissed off by the subject line of Sgt. Sean's latest email to him: "WHERE ARE WE AT ON THE SPREE KILLINGS?"

*Where are **we** at? Who the hell are **we**?* Clayton thought. Clay knew damned well where he was at on the spree killings, but as far as his supervisor went, Clay had no idea where he got off saying "we." Sean had only recently returned from a month of paternity leave and hadn't been seen in person since, leading Clay to have even more derisive thoughts about Sean. *Paternity leave. What a load of horseshit. What did the Boy Wonder have to do with having the baby? What a pansy.*

Sean's email explained in detail just how much pressure he had been under since his return from baby leave. Sean said he was taking it from all sides: the media, the public, and his captain. He needed "to be brought up to speed on the case's progress." The email explained that Officer (Lisa) Bennington would now be assigned to assist in the investigation full-time, as he considered this to be the highest priority for their detachment. Nowhere in his correspondence did Super Sarge say a word about himself helping on the case nor of Clay's request for assistance from SIU.

SIU is the department's Special Investigative Unit, which is made up of a group of five to seven detectives who are primarily tasked with

22

investigating large-scale illegal fish and wildlife trafficking cases. SIU detectives not only receive additional specialized training beyond what fish and wildlife officers receive, but they also have access to all kinds of secret squirrel equipment. Although Clay had never seen any of it, he had been told this group of detectives had remote surveillance cameras in every size and shape, as well as all kinds of other specialized equipment. If nothing else, Clay could really use a few of those cameras to place along forest roads to at least get a record of which vehicles had been up specific roads. But since first requesting SIU's assistance two months ago, Clay had not yet received a response.

Often times Clay was very thankful to be so far away from the headquarters office in Olympia. Headquarters was 317 miles from Clay's home, resulting in Clay's belief that headquarters didn't even know who the officers in Okanogan County were. Clay often told his co-workers that he doubted anyone in the headquarters office could pick out Okanogan County on a map, but that was just the way they all liked it—all except for Sean, who was starved for the chief's attention. Clay began his reply to Sean.

> Sean: While you were off, I had two more critters go down: a decent-sized male black bear (found about three weeks ago) and a large-bodied mule deer buck, which I processed yesterday. The bear was killed up Carter Pass, while the buck was found just off the 2310 road. Got a real good bullet from the bear and a useless bullet from the buck. Nothing was missing from the buck, and only the paws were taken from the bear. No meat was taken from either animal. Still no suspects. I am at the point now that when we come up with a suspect or suspects, we will have a ton of physical evidence to tie back to them, but finding them is proving to be tough.

23

I will give Lisa a call in the morning and arrange to meet up with her to formulate a plan, but I could sure use more help. I also need to meet up with the new taxidermist in town and pick his brain. Did you ever get ahold of SIU, and if so, what did they have to say about my request?

Lisa was fairly new to Okanogan County. She had recently transferred from Redmond (a suburb of Seattle) to Omak because her wife had accepted a deputy sheriff's position with the Okanogan County Sheriff's Office. Lisa was twenty-eight years old and had been a WDFW (Washington Department of Fish and Wildlife) officer for just over four years. Clay had never worked with a female officer before and, to his knowledge, had never worked with a gay officer either. At first, Clay was not sure what to make of her, but over the last few months, he had grown to consider Lisa a damned good game warden and friend. Lisa's law enforcement style was totally different than what Clay was accustomed to, but it worked.

For one thing, Lisa was always "running" everybody and everything. Whether it be by radio through dispatch (Washington Fish and Wildlife Officers use WA State Patrol dispatch) or on her MDT (Mobile Data Terminal- Laptop), she seemed to run stolen checks on every vehicle she saw and warrant checks on damned near every individual she came in contact with. Because of this, Lisa made a lot of trips to the jail with suspects who had outstanding warrants, but she also made a lot of good fish and wildlife cases.

Lisa was originally from Camas, Washington (a bedroom community for Portland, Oregon), and had zero hunting and fishing experience when she was hired. Clay had noticed a lot of the newer officers had never hunted or fished in their lives, putting them at a

24

disadvantage due to their lack of understanding of the activities they were now mandated to regulate. These "kids" who found themselves in this position had two choices: learn as much as they could as quickly as possible or stay status quo. Those new, young officers who were highly self-motivated and smart dove in and learned the ropes quickly, thus blending in with the rest of the game warden world. The other group of new officers, whether because of lack of motivation or interest, seemed quite happy to go the rest of their careers, knowing little about the profession they had chosen. They survived on a diet of traffic infractions, litter cases, and "general authority" criminal cases to keep their stats up. These kids had learned that for the same pay as the bust-ass real game wardens received, they could run around dispensing piddly little traffic tickets, thus keeping their numbers up and making everyone happy.

Fortunately for Clay, Lisa (who was the closest thing he had to a partner) was one who dove in headfirst, absorbing information like a sponge. Transferring in from the overcrowded urban environment of Redmond, Clay hadn't expected much from Lisa when he first learned she was taking the vacant officer position in Omak, but he had been pleasantly surprised. While she still had a lot to learn, she was highly motivated, smart, and set high expectations for herself. Lisa had once told Clay that her goal wasn't to be the best female officer in the state but to be the best all-around game warden in the state. One thing that made things a lot easier for Lisa was that she filled the spot vacated by Officer Jay Harlow when he retired. Jay was a good reminder that not all of the game wardens from the good old days were valuable, as he had been widely considered to be a ROD (retired on duty) for the

25

majority of his career. It's always easier to be the one replacing a worthless drone than it is to replace a rock star.

While Lisa did a great job filling in the gaps in her knowledge of fish and wildlife, one disadvantage she was aware of was her size. While not a tall man (Clay stood at only 5'09"), few men would want to take him on. Clay was one of those men who looked like a Rottweiler on two feet. With a barrel chest, large muscular arms, almost no neck, and a head the size of a buffalo's, he was one guy most people would rather have as a friend than an enemy.

On the other hand, Lisa was about as physically intimidating as a rabbit. While she kept in top physical condition, her 5'04" 125 lb. frame didn't exactly make bad guys quiver in their boots. In the academy, Lisa's DT (defensive tactics) instructor drilled it into their heads that those officers who faced opponents far larger/stronger than themselves had to be better at de-escalation than their linebacker-sized counterparts. The physically smaller officers would need to be ready to go with their issued defensive weapons (taser, pepper spray, baton, or firearm) earlier than the larger/stronger officers. Simply put, the smaller officers, whether male or female, had to depend on their brains and their mouths more than their more physically formattable co-workers. Lisa had never been in a fight and hoped to keep it that way. Clay, she knew, had been in two all-out fights in his career, and many years before Lisa had been hired, he had lost one of them pretty severely, landing him in the hospital for over a week.

As Clay got to really know Lisa, he realized how much adversity she had already faced in her career and life in general. He also understood how much adversity she had to face in her future.

26

Lisa's father had disavowed her when he learned she was gay. She and her wife had moved to a very conservative, redneck county to work in male-dominated careers. Really, that alone proved she was tough. Once Lisa and Emily had settled into their new home, a mini ranch near Tonasket (about halfway between Omak and Oroville), they began their search for a church to join. After attending services in a half-dozen different churches, they chose the First Christian Church of Okanogan. Sadly, the First Christian Church of Okanogan didn't choose the women. After attending just a couple of services, the pastor invited the ladies in for a chat, at which time he declared they could never be parish members in the church because of the "immoral lifestyle they had chosen." Apparently, both Lisa and Emily pointed out the hypocrisy of this decision to the pastor, but it fell on the deaf ears of an ignorant man.

Clay still vividly remembered his wife Karen's reaction to the news that two young law enforcement officers were banned from a Christian church because of their sexuality. Karen went nuts, throwing out terms such as lawsuit, discrimination, and even a swear word or two. One thing led to another until Karen and Clay's little Oroville Community Church proudly had two new members. Although Clay didn't really attend services anymore, Karen was a regular and provided Emily and Lisa a familiar face at most services. The two women were soon fully adopted by almost the entire congregation, especially Clay and Karen's good friends Moe and Garma Ohmar.

27

CHAPTER 4

Clay and Lisa arrived at the restaurant in their separate patrol trucks within minutes of each other. One of Clay's favorite greasy spoon diners, the Sportsman's Bar and Grill, offered a great breakfast but not the privacy needed for their planning session. Lisa and Clay had planned on leaving one of their trucks behind after breakfast and jumping in one truck together for the serious conversations while doing a bit of patrolling.

Oroville has a population of around 1,700, and on this day, it seemed to Clay as if half of them were in the Sportsman's. The local game wardens in a small-town café meant a chance for the entire town to ask dumb questions and to advise him just how he should do his job. Then there was the ever so funny, "Hey Tom, don't tell him about the deer we shot last night. Hah, hah," or the, "Did you get them guys killing all the deer yet?" which was always followed by, "I could catch 'em in a week if I had a badge."

As Lisa and Clay slipped into a booth near the back, Lisa took the seat with her back to the wall. When she first arrived in the county, everyone had to stare at the "girl game warden," but at least in Oroville, pretty much everyone had met Lisa through the church or in the field. While the department, at that time, had close to a dozen female officers, Lisa was the first this community had ever seen.

After the locals had their chance to talk to the game wardens, the wardens ordered breakfast. They held the conversation to general small talk throughout the meal.

28

On the way out, after saying goodbye to the entire restaurant, Lisa asked Clay, "Why don't we take your truck? You know the area better than me."

As soon as Clay had the truck running and heading out of the parking lot, Lisa lowered her voice into her best Sgt. Sean impersonation, "So, where are we at on the spree killings? We need to get this wrapped up, you know. I'm under a lot of pressure here."

While extending his right-middle finger, Clay responded, "Bite me, Sean," as they both laughed their way down Main Street.

"Have I ever taken you up Agate Creek?" Clay asked.

"When I first got here, I think maybe you took me up there," Lisa replied.

"All right, let's go check that area out first. It's one of the drainages that seems to have been hit the worst," Clay added.

Agate Creek Road is located about six miles south of Oroville and headed west into an absolute maze of roads in the Okanogan National Forest. Clay had processed the kill scenes of four of the poached animals in this area and had placed one of his personally owned trail cameras on one of the spur roads off which two animals had been poached.

"You know, during an average year, I am probably made aware of a dozen or so big game animals being poached, but almost all of those are during a big game hunting season, not like these," Clay stated. "You know. Guys shooting a mountain lion without a tag while they are up deer hunting or some idiot trying to sneak an elk out during deer

29

season. That kind of thing. Not this kinda stuff. This killing shit just to kill it doesn't make much sense. Don't get me wrong, we have our fair share of poaching rats in this county, but I can't think of anyone who would do this kinda stuff.

"How many total do you have in your area now?" Clay asked.

"You know that's not a simple question for me to answer. In this same time period, from almost a year to now, I only have five kills I would consider to be similar, but my low numbers may be because you are finding a higher percentage of the carcasses killed in your area than I am," Lisa answered. "Look at the Sportsman's this morning. You are the king of Oroville. Hell, half of the people in there this morning came up to talk to you even if they didn't really have anything to talk to you about. There's no doubt the community here loves and supports you and would be happy to pass on information to you. But for me, it's a different story. I haven't been here very long, and I don't fit the community's image of a game warden. It's gonna take me a while longer, but I'll get there eventually. Right now, I'm not hearing much down south."

"Don't feel too bad about the lack of calls. If it weren't for Moe, I wouldn't have found half of these. He's always out in the woods, taking wildlife pictures and finding new places to fly-fish. Moe has found and turned in more of these than anyone else. Moe's kind of my one-man posse. Now that you are officially assigned to working this case as your highest priority, I'm hoping we can make some progress," Clay added. "You know, you have the five, and I have thirty-three, but we don't know crap about the neighboring counties and regions. We need to get Boy Wonder to send out an email to all the eastern

30

Washington regions, asking if they have had any similar occurrences. It would say a lot if this was occurring outside of our county at the same rate and during the same time period."

As she took notes, Lisa asked, "What are the similarities between the kills you have found so far?"

"That's what frustrates me the most. There aren't any real similarities that I have seen. You and I have recovered bullets from numerous different calibers—from .22's to .30 cal. The footprint and tire track impressions are different from scene to scene. About a third of my critters have been ungulates (deer, elk, or moose), while the other two-thirds are bears. Sometimes the backstraps (the most desirable cut of meat on a game animal) are missing. Sometimes the head is missing, but most times, the whole animal was just left behind. I have had bears where all four paws have been removed, while others were fully intact. The only real thing these kill scenes have in common is very little evidence. We haven't recovered a single shell casing from any of the kill scenes. We don't have a single witness. Not even a beer can with fingerprints. Nothing.

"I made a map, which I should have brought this morning. I have marked the location of every kill we have found so far. I will scan it and email it to you tonight."

Lisa asked, "Is there any pattern to the times and dates of these incidents?"

"That's a tough one to narrow down, too, because in most cases, these poached animals were not found and turned over to me until they had created a gathering of scavengers (crows, eagles, magpies, bears,

31

and coyotes) and had started to melt into a goo. I'm not sure what time of day this stuff is happening, whether it's broad daylight or three a.m. I've tried varying my patrol hours, but it hasn't produced yet. The only pattern I have seen is that the poachings don't seem to occur during any of the modern firearms seasons, only before and after, and they totally stopped in winter and started back up in spring," Clay explained.

"I wonder if that means the suspect(s) are hunting guides or something like that, and they are too busy during the major hunting seasons to get out and do this?" Lisa asked.

Clay spoke up, "Nah, I think it's probably a matter of privacy or lack thereof. During the major hunting seasons for deer or elk, there are tons of hunters out crawling over every inch of ground. Just too many witnesses. Hunters usually make pretty good witnesses because they know which seasons are open and what the regulations are, so they are more likely to recognize a violation when they see one."

"See something. Say something," Lisa announced. "We can steal the line from the Homeland Security ads. Speaking of which, what about using the media to stir up tips?"

"You already know my opinion of the media, especially here." Clay continued, "I know they have already had a couple of little blurbs about this in the paper and even found Sergeant Sean to interview, but I'm not sure how speaking to the media right now would help. People already know that if they find a poached animal to call us."

"Okay, but I think we should brief the Sheriff's office, the local troopers, and the Forest Service LEOs (Law Enforcement Officers) on

32

what we have and how they can help," Lisa offered. "I will be glad to handle that if you want, seeing as how much you love speaking in front of groups."

"It would be my pleasure to pass that duty on to you. You're perfect for it," Clay said with a grin. "I will even tag along for moral support."

To that, Lisa only needed a two-word response, "Gee, thanks!"

"One other thing I have been meaning to do is to go into the new taxidermy shop in Oroville, meet the taxidermist, and do a surprise inspection. I don't have any reason to think this guy is connected, but he did arrive and set up shop after this all started," Clay said. "I've got a copy of his taxidermy license on my clipboard, and it's about time we met anyway. I have stopped in at his shop a couple of times, but it was always closed. I know where the guy lives because I have seen his silver Toyota Tacoma parked at his shop and in front of a house on 17th avenue. Guy's name is Matthew Davis."

"Have you run him?" asked Lisa as she turned Clay's laptop stand toward the passenger's seat.

"Nah, I know how much you enjoy doing that, so I left him all for you," Clay responded with a smile.

Taxidermists in Washington are tightly regulated businesses since they commercially deal in wildlife. The rules and regulations for taxidermists and their record-keeping requirements aren't complex but are often violated. Unscrupulous taxidermists have been known to take in animals that are illegal to possess, such as eagles and owls, and often

33

keep two sets of books. These illegal taxidermists, desperate for business, will mount illegal wildlife in a separate location (many times in their garage at home) and thus can keep their "open to the public" shop above-board and legal.

Taxidermists vary from true artisans to hacks. There is no training requirement nor any certificate of competency, so basically, anyone can call themselves a taxidermist as long as they have a business license and a taxidermist license. Either way, they do need to have their required paperwork in order.

Taxidermists can legally work on many different game animals if they were taken legally and are accompanied by the appropriate tag and license numbers and seals. Still, they can't buy or sell many of them. So, in the vast majority of cases, taxidermists return the mounted animal to the same person who harvested it. Wildlife items that are illegal to buy or sell are enumerated in the hunting regulations, as are the penalties for trafficking in those animal parts. All are felony-level crimes.

"Shit, no warrants. I was hoping to take someone to jail today," Lisa announced as her warrant check request came back. "He came from someplace named Grass Valley, California, has a prior game violation for unlawful transportation of wildlife, and has had a Washington driver's license since last November," she continued.

"Well, sorry to ruin your day, but there is always hope," Clay said. "I've seen him driving around town, and he's your kinda boy: long stringy hair and lots of tats. Looks like a skinny biker without the bike."

"How about trail cameras? We could put up cameras on roads where we are having the most problems," Lisa inquired.

"I have a personally owned trail camera up right now on a spur road off Agate Creek," Clay explained. "I've had it up for about two weeks now, but nothing has shown up. I'm not even sure what I'm looking for, but I have written down the license numbers of every vehicle that went up that road, but none of them looked like hunters to me. I asked Sean to request help and cameras from SIU, but I haven't heard back yet."

"If you want, I will stay on Sean about SIU and the cameras," Lisa offered.

Clay replied, "Nah, I've got it. I figure that if I don't get an answer by the end of the week, I will go to the top and call the SIU captain directly. That otta light a fire under them."

"Yeah, circumventing the chain of command has always worked so well for you. Why not do it again?" Lisa jokingly added.

As they headed back to Oroville to conduct the taxidermy inspection, Lisa asked, "So where are Moe and Garma originally from? I'm guessing India."

"They are really interesting people. The Ohmars are from Myanmar, which is somewhere around India. I know he said they had elephants there. Anyway, Moe was a police commander for the Myanmar National Police Force. I guess he even worked elephant poaching cases occasionally. I know you've met their girls at church, but they are why Moe and Garma moved to the United States." Clay

35

went on, "At some point, around 2015, Myanmar got a new president or supreme leader or whatever the hell they call him, and the guy immediately ordered the extermination of Hindu people. I guess government forces executed over 24,000 people."

"Moe is not the kind of guy to have anything to do with mass murder, and he refused to have any part of the genocide," Clay explained, "which I guess didn't go over too well with his bosses. So literally, in the middle of the night, they packed up their valuables and fled to India. From India, they moved to Canada. They first lived in Penticton, B.C. (only an hour north of Oroville), but they only stayed in Penticton for a couple of months before moving to Oroville, where they bought the only gas station/mini-mart in town. He named the business Moe-Mart."

"How could they afford to buy a gas station and mini-mart?" Lisa inquired.

"They aren't poor. Garma was the head of nursing at their largest hospital, and Moe was a police commander in charge of hundreds of officers. He graduated from Oxford and then attended the FBI academy, so he was a big deal back in his homeland. Because he quit and left Myanmar, I guess his extended family back there has been subjected to some pretty vicious harassment, which is why they are working so hard to get them moved over here too. It's kinda sad to see them go from the lives they had in Myanmar to selling beer and cigarettes in Oroville, but it seems to work for them, and they are safe and happy," Clay explained. "Since they moved here, they have brought over several family members, most of whom now live in

36

Penticton. I guess it's easier to first immigrate to Canada and then work on the process of coming to the U.S."

"Sounds like the great American success story to me," Lisa said.

As they rounded the corner onto 12th Avenue from behind the grocery store, Clay could already see the silver Toyota parked in front of the taxidermy shop.

"He's there." Clay sang out, "Check out his sign."

The new wooden sign had a logo of three W's all butted up against each other in a line, looking like a silhouette of mountain peaks. Underneath the logo, the name was spelled out: "Wildlife, Water, and Wings Taxidermy."

"Let's hit it," Clay decreed.

As they walked toward the front door, Clay heard some unfamiliar music. "What is that garbage?" he muttered to Lisa.

"Where you been? That's "No Guidance" by Chris Brown. Like it? Now I know what to get for your birthday," Lisa said with a grin.

The taxidermy shop had taken over the space from a failed video rental business. It consisted of one wide-open 24' x 18' single room with a tiny bathroom in the very back. The store's back door had a newly installed metal mesh screen over the glass and a very serious-looking deadbolt lock.

Fortunately, Mr. Davis had remotely turned down the "music" as Lisa and Clay entered the shop. Taxidermy shops all stink, and this one was no different. The combination of rotting meat, tanning

37

chemicals, and Bondo (a two-part plastic filler) makes for a very unique odor. Like every taxidermy shop they had ever been in, the shop was cluttered with polyurethane forms (made from molded foam), hides laying in a pile of rock salt, mounting stands, and antlers. Davis had been working on mounting a whitetail deer and was in the process of pinning the hide in place when the wardens arrived.

Introductions were made with handshakes all around.

"In addition to introducing ourselves to you, we need to conduct a quick taxidermy inspection. I assume you have been through this before somewhere?" Clay asked.

"Nope, this is the first shop I have worked in under my own license. Not too long ago, I went to taxidermy school in Spokane and worked in another guy's shop, helping out and getting some experience before I branched out on my own," the taxidermist replied.

"So why Oroville, out of all the places you could have gone?" Lisa asked.

"It's pretty simple, really. When I was in taxidermy school, I would take off on weekends and just go explore," Mr. Davis explained. "One day, I drove up here and couldn't believe it. The area is beautiful, uncrowded, has tons of wildlife, and didn't have a taxidermist in town. Then the bonus was this shop. I pay $225 a month in rent for this whole shop. California sucks, and I couldn't wait to get out. I'm never going back."

Lisa and Clay then checked his receipt book and records to make sure they all lined up with the wildlife he had in his shop. Every

38

wildlife item had to be entered and accounted for, including the name, address, hunting license number, etc. They looked through the three chest freezers he had, as well as at the hides he had tanning and in salt.

"Why's this guy's deer tag stapled to the receipt?" Clay asked.

"Yeah, that was one of the first ones I took in, and I thought I had to have the actual tag with the horns. I called Olympia about it and was told the tag had to remain with the meat, and all I needed was the guy's tag number. My bad," said Matt.

Other than the tag, everything was in order, and they said their goodbyes. As Matt walked them to the door, Lisa pointed at one of his many tattoos, one with a snarling pit bull with the words "Mad Dog" at the bottom, and she asked, "What's with the Mad Dog tat?"

"Oh, that was in my wild days. My buddies always called me Mad Dog because my initials are MD. So, you know, like MD 20/20, Mad Dog." Matt explained.

"Something's not right with that guy. He just gave me the creeps," Lisa announced as they got back into Clay's truck.

"I don't know about the creeps, but one thing I don't like is the company he keeps," Clay noted.

"Why, what company he keeps?"

"In his receipt book. Damned near every piece of shit poacher in the county has been doing business with Mr. Davis there," Clay proclaimed. "For a guy who's only been here for a few months, he sure did find himself a bunch of shitheads to hang out with."

Lisa asked, "You said he got here after the spree killings started, but just how much after?"

CHAPTER 5

In Washington State, the state forests are managed by the Washington Department of Natural Resources, referred to as the DNR. Grant Saunders had been working for the DNR for over thirty-three years. He started as a forest technician and found himself running heavy equipment for the better part of his career. Today was day one of his quarterly road grading job on the Clear Creek Road. He had "walked" the Cat 140M AWD motor grader up the road while towing his work truck behind. Like a hundred times before, Grant planned to leave his truck at an old DNR gravel pit, the same place he would leave the grader when he took his truck home tonight. The project would only take him two days, so he wasn't too worried about the grader getting vandalized out by itself for one night. *One nice thing about living here is there's no crime*, Grant thought as he saw his turnoff just ahead.

As he turned into the nice flat surface of the old pit, he immediately noticed the garbage someone had dumped. "God damned slobs," he muttered as he climbed down from the grader's cab. "Looks like a body all wrapped up like that."

The closer Grant got to the garbage, the more concerned he grew. It did look like a body wrapped up in the blue tarp. "Oh, man," Grant said aloud as he took out his pocketknife, "please don't be what I think it is."

Before cutting the tarp, Grant poked it with his boot just to make sure something wasn't alive in there. Starting at the smaller end of the tapered tarp, he didn't bother cutting the duct tape but just cut a 4" slit

41

to take a peek in. As he inserted his fingers into the hole he had just cut, he had an awful feeling. Grant pulled the tarp apart enough to see in.

Stumbling backward, he fell flat on his back, reeling from the sight of the human foot. It was a very small human foot. "Oh my God. It's a kid," Grant choked the words out.

With no cell service in the area, Grant sprinted for his truck and its radio. Forgetting all radio protocol, he shouted into the mic, "I'm up at the Clear Creek Pit, and there's a dead kid wrapped up in a tarp up here. Get someone here now! Now!" Grant sat in his truck and cried. He cried for the first time since he didn't know how long. "What the hell is wrong with people?" he asked himself.

After what seemed like an eternity, the first responder arrived. It was Deputy Mark Hendricks. Deputy Hendricks had been on the job for a little over three years, and he had already seen and experienced plenty, but he was sure hoping this call would be a false alarm.

The deputy introduced himself to Grant, "I'm Deputy Mark Hendricks. So, what have we got here?"

"What you've got is a dead kid. Some piece of shit killed this kid wrapped him up, and dumped him here," Grant explained in a shaky voice.

Deputy Hendricks was trying to stay calm and professional, but inside he just wanted to go home—home to his kids and his family.

"I cut a hole at the bottom, so I could see in," Grant yelled as he stayed back by his truck, "but I didn't touch nothing."

42

Hendricks first took photos of the entire gravel pit area, followed by close-ups of the rolled-up tarp. He then donned a pair of latex gloves and knelt next to the tarp. The tarp had been wrapped around the body, if there was a body in there, then taped all the way around in four different spots. There were no markings or other identifying details on the tarp.

Deputy Hendricks moved his sunglasses to the top of his ballcap and then leaned in to look at the opening cut by Grant. "Ah shit. I was hoping you were wrong," Hendricks said to Grant.

Almost immediately after Deputy Hendricks touched the victim's ankle, he felt the cold. The body was significantly cooler than the ambient air temperature. The kid was definitely dead. He thought long and hard about what to do next. Before he called into dispatch, he had to make 100% sure the kid was dead. Nothing would be worse than to leave the kid wrapped up while he waited for assistance, only to later find the kid suffocated while the deputy waited there.

Now it was time for the deputy to cut his own hole in the tarp, this time at the other end, the head end. Using his Benchmade tactical knife, Deputy Hendricks cut a small hole in the tarp. Before spreading open the gap he had cut, Hendricks mentally prepared himself for what he was about to see. The deputy then began pulling open the tarp, revealing not a kid but a petite adult female. He guessed her to be around 30 years old. *She was probably a head-turner when she was all dressed up*, he thought to himself.

"What a shame. This young woman was murdered and dumped like this," Hendricks said to no one in particular.

43

After feeling for a pulse, Deputy Hendricks snapped a few more photos before getting on the county radio and advising dispatch to send detectives. He held off on describing what he had seen as it seemed that half of the population of Okanogan County had police scanners.

Mr. Saunders asked Deputy Hendricks if it was okay for him to leave now, and deciding to err on the side of caution, Hendricks told Grant, "I would like you to stick around until the detectives arrive. Then it will be up to them."

"Can I at least go down the road, just around this first corner? I've just gotta get out of here. I can't breathe here," Grant replied.

"That's fine. If you want, just hang out around the corner, and maybe you can even direct the others in this way," Hendricks answered.

Deputy Hendricks didn't like being left alone with the body. It gave him the creeps. *Who would do this, and why?* he thought. *Damn, I wish the detectives would get here soon.*

About 45 minutes after he had notified dispatch of the body, a detective and a uniformed sergeant both arrived. They quickly took short verbal statements from both Grant Saunders and Deputy Hendricks before cutting them both loose. "Mr. Saunders, we want to thank you for your assistance. Here's my card. We would like to get you to come in to provide us with a written statement in the next two days if that will work for you," Detective Olmsted said.

"I'll give you a call tomorrow to work out the details, but right now, I just want to go home," replied Grant.

44

The detective and the Sergeant then went about the task of documenting everything. They took dozens of photos. They took measurements of the gravel pit, how far the body was from the road, and every other detail needed to be able to recreate the scene. While waiting for the coroner to arrive, the men began a systematic search of the area around the body, looking for any physical evidence. Being a gravel pit, it was littered with hundreds, if not thousands, of spent .22 casings and shotgun hulls. There was broken glass everywhere from the beer bottles shattered by bullets fired by the very slobs who left this crap behind for someone else to deal with. The detective/sergeant team knew they would be out here for hours to come and would need more help.

When the coroner arrived in her van, Cricket (still wrapped in the blue tarp) was lifted onto a large white cotton sheet. The coroner explained that the sheet would capture and contain any forensics evidence that might fall off the tarp or the body. The body was then loaded on a gurney and taken away, leaving the Sergeant and detective to continue processing the scene. A second detective was told by radio to meet the coroner in Omak to assist with the examination.

Coroner Kim Spooner graduated from Washington State University with a degree in criminology and then began her career in government service as a legal assistant with the Okanogan County Prosecuting Attorney's Office. That position gave her a real-world look at the field of forensics science, which interested her a whole lot more than reading, writing, and reviewing legal documents all day long. Two years ago, when she learned the elected coroner at the time was retiring, she set her sights on his post, which she then won in an unopposed election.

Since Kim was not a medical doctor, she contracted with the Omak General Hospital for formal medical autopsies. In the more complex cases, she would also request the assistance of trained forensics medical examiners from Western Washington.

Once the wrapped body was placed on the spotless stainless-steel examination table, Kim began opening the white sheet it was contained in. At the same time, Detective David Carpenter took yet more photos. With the sheet laid open and the tarp-wrapped body still on top of it, the two began a slow and thorough examination of the tarp and duct tape. The duct tape was your standard silver-gray duct tape—nothing unusual. The tarp appeared to be well used, with several frayed spots. As they were moving down the length of the tarp, Spooner pointed out a reddish-brown, dried, and flaky spot about the diameter of a pencil's eraser, saying, "Whoa, what's this?"

Spooner and Carpenter then took turns inspecting the stain with a magnifying glass. "Looks like it could be blood," Carpenter said.

"Well, let's find out," answered Kim. Kim explained to Detective Carpenter, "We normally use what's called a phenolphthalein test, to first determine if a sample is blood or not, before we use the ABA Hematrace immunochromatographic test strip to determine if it's human blood."

"If the "immeno chromo" thing tells if it's human blood, why not just start with it?" asked Carpenter.

46

"Money. The Hematrace test is very expensive, so we use them sparingly," she answered.

Using a scalpel, Kim removed a tiny flake of the stain and touched it to the phenolphthalein swab. Almost instantly, the swap turned pink. "We have blood," Kim announced.

The ABA Hematrace strip looks like a home early pregnancy test. It has a small hole at one end to put the sample in and a long strip above it with the markings "C" for control and "T" for test. Once the suspect sample is placed in the hole, the results come quickly. If the sample is human blood, both the "C" and "T" areas will show purple bands next to them.

Within seconds of Kim placing a tiny sample in the Hematrace, a bar appeared adjacent to the "C" on the strip, but even after 10 minutes, the "T" bar remained blank.

"Well, it's blood, but it sure isn't human blood," Kim observed.

Kim then dabbed the remainder of the mystery blood onto a moistened sterile swab. "I don't know if you want it, but here is the rest of that bloodstain," Kim said as she handed the swab to Detective Carpenter. "I kind of doubt it has anything to do with her death, but it's still evidence," she continued.

Next came the duct tape. Using blunt-nosed medical scissors, Kim carefully cut the four different wraps of duct tape. Apparently, duct tape doesn't stick very well to plastic tarps because once the tape strips were cut, they peeled off easily. These, too, went into evidence bags.

47

"I will get these to the crime lab to see if they can get any usable prints," Detective Carpenter said.

If they didn't know better, they probably would have thought Cricket was just sleeping because she didn't show any sign of trauma as she was released from the tarp.

Although this wasn't Detective Carpenter's first autopsy, he still felt a little embarrassed about undressing the victim. Most of the disrobing procedure was done with scissors, but for some items, they simply slid the clothing off. To minimize his involvement in the undressing procedure, Carpenter silently volunteered to search and inspect the clothing items as they came off.

Her face wasn't familiar to either the detective or the coroner. She had no tattoos, no identification, and no identifying features other than being petite, blonde, and attractive.

Carpenter's search of her clothing produced only one thing—a small zip-lock jewelry bag containing a brown powder. "Looks like we have some heroin here," he said as he held the bag up for the coroner.

"That explains these," Kim said as she pointed to the line of needle marks up Cricket's left arm. "What a shame. Just a waste of a life. Unfortunately, we see way too many dead bodies with track marks from slamming (injecting)."

After completing the search of her clothing and finding nothing but the drugs, Carpenter said, "About done here. No more blood or really anything other than the dope." He then began bagging all the

48

clothing in paper evidence bags. When all the clothing had been removed from the stainless-steel table, Carpenter noticed something. The exam table had two black hairs on the surface. The hairs were three to four inches long and almost jet black.

"Check this out," Carpenter told Kim. "I found these on the table. They had to have come off her clothing. Maybe these came from the killer. Could be an early break in the case."

"Let me have a look," Kim said as she reached for a pair of forceps.

Placing one of the hairs under a microscope, Kim's head swiveled back and forth between her laptop and her microscope. "The only way this hair came from the killer is if a bear killed her, wrapped her up in a tarp, and taped it closed. What you've got here is the hair from an Ursus Americanus: the American Black Bear. This is a first for me."

"Let's take another look at the tarp," Carpenter suggested.

They spread the tarp out on the same white sheet and, this time, paid more attention to the inside of the tarp. Sure enough, there were more reddish-brown stains and several more black hairs, all of which they then collected.

"Frigging weird" was all the detective could come up with.

Going back to the body, Kim continued her external examination. She rolled the victim's fingerprints onto a stiff print card and handed it to Detective Carpenter, and she then drew blood, which she kept under her control.

49

"The doc won't be able to complete the medical exam until tomorrow, so if you need to go, I've got it from here," Kim advised.

"Sounds good. I've had enough fun for one day. Please call me as soon as you know anything," the detective replied.

Kim's two-word response was, "Of course."

CHAPTER 6

Four days after last hearing from Super Sarge, Clay received a forwarded email from him labeled: "Fwd: Your Wish is Our Command."

"What the hell is that supposed to mean?" muttered Clay to himself as he opened the email. When he was done reading, he shouted out to Karen, "Hey, check this out. The wonder boy actually did something. Looks like we are getting some of the help from SIU we have been asking for."

> Sgt. Dresken: We received your request for assistance and would be more than happy to provide you with the equipment you asked for to help y'all catch your spree killers. Please ask Officer Newberry to give me a call at his convenience so that we can discuss the details. I will be available until late Wednesday (I'm heading out on vacation with the family before school starts). If we don't connect by then, tell him to call Detective Robbins, who will be in charge while I'm gone. I wish we could spare the manpower to send you bodies to help, but we are swamped right now.
>
> Take care and happy hunting. Captain Aaron Hamlin

"Well, call him. It sounds like you are going to get some new toys," Karen suggested.

Clay had known Aaron for around thirty years since they had gone to the academy together—back when dinosaurs roamed the earth. With a gray beard, matching ponytail, and standing over 6'04", Aaron was as laid back as anyone could ever be. Aaron used to say that after his three divorces, he learned to quit worrying about the things he couldn't change. Aaron was always one step ahead of everyone else and was one of the most intelligent people Clay had ever met, but he sure did have trouble staying married for any length of time.

Clay decided to speed things up and call Aaron. "Hey Aaron, this is Clay. Thanks for getting back to us."

"Yeah, sorry about the delay. We have been pretty busy here, but your Sarge wouldn't let it go. I tried like hell to ignore you, but Sean sent us about a dozen emails and left me a couple of phone messages. But like I said, we have been swamped," Hamlin responded. "So, I got the gist of things from Sean, but why don't you fill me in on what you've got going on there."

Clay took the time to go over everything he could think of. He explained it all the best he could remember and then waited to hear what Aaron thought.

"Okay, but you said that in your opinion, this isn't a commercial poaching operation. How did you come to that conclusion?" Hamlin asked.

"Because on almost all of the animals, the poachers didn't take any part of the critters. Just left them there to rot," Clay answered.

"But you said about two-thirds of your poached animals are bears. I assume you've checked to see if the gallbladders were still intact?" Hamlin asked.

"Well, not really," Clay responded. "By the time most of these were turned into me, they had all been dead long enough to start turning to goo. I dug for bullets on every carcass the metal detector said had a bullet in it, but I guess I didn't specifically look to see if the gall was there or not. I never saw any open cuts on any of the bear carcasses, but as I said, most were at the goo stage."

"A guy that knows what he is doing can make a deep cut about ten inches long to get the gall out of a bear. I've seen some bear where you couldn't find the cut unless you looked carefully," Aaron explained. "On the next bear you find dead, take a good look for the gall. You know where it is, right?"

"Yeah, but bear gall is used by Chinese and Koreans, right?" Clay asked.

"You are correct. There apparently are a few other cultures who use bear gall, but certainly Chinese and Koreans make up 95% of the consumers," Aaron replied.

"So, I have two problems with the commercial bear gall angle," Clay expounded. "First, I'm not sure we even have one single Asian family in the entire county. I mean, we don't even have a Chinese restaurant. Secondly, that wouldn't explain the dead deer and elk. I've never heard of a deer gall black market."

"Hey, it's just something to keep in mind," Hamlin replied. "All right, tell me if you agree with the equipment wish list your sergeant sent me. We have you down for six covert cameras, and you can have all of them for a couple of months. We also added two GPS trackers for when you have your suspects narrowed down, a set of NVGs (Night Vision Goggles), and lastly, a 2008 Ford F-150. The truck is on loan, so try not to break it. Sean thought it might be better for y'all to

53

use a plain unmarked truck for your sneaking around, and we just happened to have this one available. Obviously, it won't do you much good if you park it in front of your house. Will that work for ya?" Aaron asked.

"Hell yeah. That's awesome. Way better than I expected, but now I have to take back some of the things I said about you. You aren't totally worthless after all," Clay joked.

Clay went on, "I'll talk to Lisa about where to leave the truck, but I'm thinking at her house or at a buddy of mine's house here. They live off the main road far enough that people couldn't see it while driving by. So, how do I get it all?"

"Let me know a day in advance, and we will meet you in Cle Elum. That should be about halfway for both of us. We will sit down with you guys for a few minutes to go over the operation of the cameras and the trackers, but they are so simple even a captain could figure them out," Hamlin stated.

"Okay. I will get ahold of Lisa and see what her schedule looks like, and then I'll get back to you or Randy Robbins. Thanks, man. I appreciate it," Clay said.

"Not a problem, buddy. Go get those assholes."

Clay's next call was to Lisa, "Looks like SIU has a whole bunch of brand-new toys just waiting for us to pick up in Cle Elum. So, what's your schedule look like for the next couple of days?"

"Wide open. I don't have anything scheduled until the weekend after next. Let's go on a road trip," Lisa exclaimed.

54

Clay answered, "Okay, I will shoot for tomorrow. I will send you a text and let you know what time we will need to leave—after I get in touch with Hamlin."

"All right. See ya tomorrow," Lisa returned.

As soon as Clay got off the phone, he shot Aaron Hamlin a simple text message, "Tomorrow works for both of us. It will take us about three hours to get to Cle Elum. Let us know if tomorrow works, and if so, what time. Clay."

Soon after, Aaron responded. "Cottage Café on 1st, at eleven a.m. You can buy us the lunch you owe us for saving your butt again. You might want to throw in a bottle of Crown, just as a thank you to us for sharing our wisdom and expertise with you. See ya then, and come in plain clothes in your POV (privately owned vehicle)."

Clay answered back. "Thanks. See ya tomorrow."

Clay's next text was to Lisa. "I'll pick you up at your place at 7:30. See ya in the morning."

Lisa replied. "Please be quiet in the morning. Emily is on swing shift this week. See ya, manana."

After Clay filled Karen in on the news of the forthcoming equipment, she advised Clay. "I hate to tell you what to do, but you really should call Sean and thank him."

"I don't know. I've always been opposed to thanking someone for doing the job they are paid to do." Clay looked up at Karen as he

55

responded and, noting her expression of dissatisfaction, added, "but I will be glad to call."

Clay poured himself another cup of coffee and then called Sean.

"Hey Sean, Clay. So, it sounds like you stayed on Aaron like stink on shit," Clay said.

"Cool. You got in touch with him then; I take it?" Sean asked.

"Yeah, I just spoke to him, and we are all set. We are gonna meet him in Cle Elum at eleven tomorrow. He is bringing us a plain unmarked truck, a bunch of cameras, a set of NVGs, and a couple of GPS trackers," said Clay. "We do need permission to go plainclothes and to get paid for mileage in my POV."

"Of-course. Do what you gotta do. All I ask of you two is just to keep me in the loop," Sean answered. "If you need anything else, you know where to find me."

"Yeah. Hey, thanks for taking care of that. You apparently asked for a couple of things I didn't even think of, but they will definitely help. We do appreciate it," Clay told Sean.

"No problem. Talk to ya later." And with that, Sean hung up.

CHAPTER 7

The four of them huddled around the cluttered coffee table, staring down at the bag of brown gold. After much discussion, it was agreed Brian would go first. After all, he's the one who took the scrap copper into Wenatchee. Over one hundred pounds of copper fetched the crew $237.43. It took the four men most of the last night to "acquire" (steal) the copper pipe and wiring from construction sites. When it was time to turn copper into gold, they went to their number one man and scored some H. Now that the work was done, it was time to party.

Brian wrapped the bootlace around his arm, just under the bicep, to get his veins to pop up. Remembering to always face the needle toward the heart, Brian picked a spot on his left forearm to slide the needle in. Before injecting, Brian first drew the syringe plunger back up, drawing a small amount of blood into the syringe and thus confirming the needle was in the vein properly.

As Brian pushed the plunger down, he could instantly feel the euphoria he had waited for. Heroin made Brian happy—at least for now. Once the heroin reached the portion of the brain called the nucleus accumbens, it interacted with the "happy hormone" dopamine. It was then the drug attached to GABAergic neurons. Without opioids, the GABA acts as a safety stop, not allowing too much dopamine to be activated. Opioid molecules override this safety stop and create bliss and happiness well beyond what our GABA cells would ever allow a body to do without it.

57

Within minutes, Brian started to slump over on the couch. His head dipped down, then jerked back up as he fought to stay conscious. Next, Brian's breathing began to slow, and his blood pressure dropped rapidly, but he was not aware of either of the issues. As his body continued to shut down, he fell into respiratory depression, finally crashing onto the floor.

All three of Brian's buddies had repeated the same process of injecting, all with the same needle, when they noticed Brian was no longer breathing and had a foamy mucus dribbling from the corner of his mouth.

"We gotta call 911. The dude is fucking dying, man," one of Brian's pals announced.

"I don't want the cops here, dumbass," said another of his crew. "We'll get busted."

"We took the same shit he did, and I ain't gonna end up dead, so I'm calling," the man said as he pulled out his cell phone and called 911.

The call went out to fire and police as a possible overdose at apartment A-21 of the Mountainview Apartment complex in Omak. The Lifeline ambulance arrived at the scene within six minutes of the call and was immediately joined by Omak PD Officer Josh Fisher and Okanogan Sheriff's Deputy Emily Bennington. All the responders carried Narcan (naloxone HCI) nasal spray since it is very effective in temporarily reversing the effects of opioids.

All four emergency responders, the ambulance had two, rushed up the stairs to apartment A-21. After knocking and announcing multiple times with no response, Officer Fisher confirmed the apartment number with dispatch before crushing the door inwards.

Once inside, they immediately noticed all four men were down. After checking their vitals, all four responders administered Narcan to each of the four men. Two men regained consciousness in a very short time period, but the other two did not respond and were then given secondary doses of the reversal drug while CPR was administered. A second ambulance arrived just after the administration of the second doses, and the crew jumped right in to assist. Patients 1 and 2 remained conscious and somewhat alert, but the others teetered on the edge, closer to death than to life.

The decision was made to transport the two critical patients right away, but that meant two of the responders would need to ride in back to continue CPR. The second ambulance was to take patients 1 and 2 with Deputy Bennington riding in the back with them. Before leaving the apartment complex, Officer Fisher called for another officer to secure the apartment since the door was not of much use anymore.

Three and a half minutes after the ambulance doors closed, they were both pulling up to the emergency entrance of the hospital, where the exhausted paramedics were relieved of their CPR duties.

"I guess you need a ride back, huh?" Officer Fisher asked Emily.

"That would be much appreciated," Emily responded.

As they pulled up alongside Emily's patrol car, Josh reached out his hand and said, "I guess we have not been formally introduced before. I'm Josh Fisher."

"Emily Bennington. Glad to meet you, even under these circumstances," she replied.

"Well, get used to it. We are in an epidemic here, and we see this same scenario at least once a week. In 2017 alone, over 40,000 Americans lost their lives to opioid overdoses," said Fisher.

By the time Emily was back on patrol, half of the four men they had taken to the hospital had been pronounced dead.

CHAPTER 8

The DJI Matrice 600 Pro hexacopter drone is a thing of beauty. She can stay aloft for 35 minutes and can cruise at 32 mph with a ceiling of over 8,000 feet. She has three separate GPS sensor modules (for redundancy), collision avoidance capability, and can still fly effectively even if one of the six motors were to quit. Best of all, the Matrice 600 can carry a payload of 13 lbs. in a container on her belly for over 12 miles on a single charge. Especially when it is flown at a low altitude, the drone is virtually invisible to radar. With the belly painted light blue and the top painted in flat black, the drone can be very difficult to spot, making it the ideal tool for discreet deliveries.

Maung loved the Matrice 600. Ever since he first started using it, he realized this was the answer to their delivery problems. He wished they had bought one of these years ago, but it was here now and working flawlessly.

Last night, he inserted a fresh battery pack and then carefully attached the package to the belly of the drone. Every time he attached the box, he gave it a couple of extra tugs to make sure it wasn't coming off. That would piss the boss off, and he was not a great guy to piss off.

Maung came by way of his eastern route today, driving west out Hwy. 3 and then south on logging roads to a nice high spot overlooking Lake Osoyoos. "She's on her way to you now," he said into his cell phone.

61

About twenty seconds after she lifted off, he couldn't hear her anymore. He lost sight of her about ten seconds after that. She would arrive at her destination in 21 minutes.

CHAPTER 9

In Clay's book, early is on time, on time is late, and late is inexcusable. He pulled up Lisa's driveway at 7:17 a.m., only to find Lisa sitting on the tailgate of her patrol truck, ready to go.

"Morning, sunshine," Clay said as Lisa climbed into the passenger seat of his personal truck.

"Didn't expect you in your personal vehicle, but it makes sense. Onward, James," Lisa said as she pointed toward the highway.

"Yeah, the secret squirrel squad doesn't like to be seen with us lowly uniforms," Clay said as they both laughed.

"So, anything new?" Lisa asked.

"Not much. I haven't found any more kills since that last mulie buck. Other than that, I've just been trying to catch up. How about you?"

"Nope, but Emily had a quad-overdose last night. Four junkies at once. Two died, and the other two are probably already back at it today. She hit one of the guys with Narcan, and he popped right back to life, but the other two never did respond to it. That was the first time she actually saved someone's life," Lisa told Clay.

"In my opinion, that Narcan shit is a waste of taxpayer's money. Junkies are supposed to die. It's natural selection. We bring them back to life, so they can commit more burglaries and thefts. What a system," Clay pointed out.

63

"I suppose if it were your son, you wouldn't feel that way," Lisa responded. "One of the guys I went to the academy with was working for Yakima P.D. when he broke his pelvis and thigh after crashing during a pursuit. A couple of surgeries later and he found himself addicted to Oxy. A couple of months after that, he ate his gun."

"Way to make me feel like an asshole," Clay sheepishly responded.

"It's just that none of us are immune to this kind of thing. It really could happen to anyone," Lisa went on. "This is an absolute epidemic, especially around here. I guess last week, the county found a young woman dead and wrapped up in a tarp—up the Clear Creek Road. Looks like another O.D."

"Yeah, sounds like the opioid problem is hitting everywhere in the U.S.," Clay responded.

Clay asked Lisa, "Hey, on a different subject, while I'm thinking of it, did you ask Sean to put out the request for information on any similar poaching incidents in eastern Washington?"

"Crap, I forgot. I'll do it right now," Lisa said as she began texting. "Done."

"So where are we gonna park this new undercover truck?" Lisa asked.

"Can't be my house. I'm too close to the main road, so I was thinking your place or Moe's," Clay answered.

"Either way is fine with me, but since you will probably use it more than me, why don't we leave it up at Moe's house so it's handy for you." Lisa went on, "I know where it is, but I've never been to Moe and Garma's house. What's it like?"

Clay shoved in a Beth Hart/Joe Bonamassa CD and adjusted the volume so that it wouldn't interfere with their conversation.

"They have a beautiful home. Not huge, but they had it custom built, and it's awesome. He has a three-car garage and a huge shop too. They sit on five fenced acres with a paved and gated driveway. Moe has a super impressive office. He has tons of photos of him with famous people, including Bill Clinton, not to mention all the awards and certificates."

"So has Moe ever considered getting into law enforcement here in some capacity?" Lisa asked.

"Nah. He would have to do our police academy from scratch and start as a rookie entry-level officer somewhere, and really, he's pretty happy with things the way they are now. His family is safe. He's making a good living, and for being only 44-years old, he goofs off almost as much as most retirees. Plus, there are the girls. He's pretty protective of them and isn't just going to leave them while he tromps off to the academy for six months. Trust me. I've tried to talk him into it, but he's not bending."

"Speaking of Moe, I better give him a call to ask him about leaving the truck at his place. I know he won't have a problem with it, but I have to ask him about giving you the gate code, too," Clay continued.

After Clay got off the phone, he said to Lisa, "No problem. He's good with it. He wants us to park on the far side of his shop, so I'll show you where. The gate code is his address backward: 1741. He only had one request, that all of us, including you and Emily, come over for a barbeque this Sunday afternoon around one pm. And, just so you know, Garma is an awesome cook. They just need us to tell him if everyone can make it, so they know how much food to prepare."

Lisa took out her phone and checked the electronic calendar before answering, "I will answer for both of us. Count us in. Just let us know what to bring."

"Cool. I will ask him, but I already know the answer. They won't let us bring anything. Maybe just bring whatever y'all want to drink."

"Sounds great. I'm looking forward to it."

"So, what does Emily think of the Okanogan Sheriff's Office?" Clay asked.

"She loves the department and the guys she works with. She said it's the most squared-away department she's ever been around," Lisa answered.

"I agree with her assessment of the S.O. (Sheriff's Office), and I'm glad she feels comfortable here," Clay added.

Twenty minutes later, Lisa was sound asleep. When your spouse works nights, it can be tough to get your own sleep in.

The "Covert Tracker 1600" GPS live tracker was shaped like a hockey puck but smaller. The nondescript dark plastic puck was smooth on one side and had a powerful magnet on the other. Once activated, the tracker provided real-time speeds, and locations of the tracker live on the user's cell phone, laptop, or tablet. "It's accurate to within 16' and will last over ten days on a single charge. We gave you two, so you can swap with a freshly charged one at will," Captain Hamlin told Lisa. Once you load the app and identify the tracker on the program, it's simply plug-and-play. Stick it to the underside of the suspect vehicle, activate it, and you're in business. Any questions?" There were none.

"I will warn you guys of two things. First, you need a warrant to place the tracker on another person's vehicle. Secondly, and most importantly, placing the tracker on a vehicle can be one of the most dangerous things we do. You will need just a few seconds to place the tracker, but that's when problems can arise," Captain Hamlin warned. "In 2009, there was a famous shooting of two police officers in New Zealand. The officers, dressed in plain clothes, were attempting to attach a tracker to a suspect's vehicle in his driveway when they were spotted by the bad guy. The suspect ran outside with a rifle and shot both officers, killing one. The suspect later claimed self-defense because he claimed to have thought the two officers were his enemies planting a bomb on his vehicle. Just be careful."

After Clay and Lisa split the lunch bill, the four said their goodbyes and headed outside.

"Why don't you follow me to Moe's? We will stuff the truck away, and I'll give you a ride home," Clay suggested.

67

CHAPTER 10

Vince Donnelly loved his new job. An unemployed logger, Vince was looking for work when this opportunity fell in his lap. One day he was over at a buddy's house, having some beers and smoking a few bowls, when his friend told Vince about the opportunity and asked if he would be interested. At first, Vince said he flat wasn't interested, but when his buddy told him about the money he had been making, it was just too tempting to pass up on.

Vince had now been at the new job for a couple of months, and the money was just as good as he had been led to believe. He had pretty much followed the law his entire life, so this still was a little strange to him, but what the hell. He was back working in the woods, climbing hills, and busting his butt at a dangerous job. Only now, it was for way better money.

These things are amazing, Vince thought as he opened the UPS package. Vince brought out six brand new Aldrich Humane Foot Snares. The snares consisted of the foot snare itself (48" of 3/16" aircraft cable), the spring snare thrower (a steel spring that launches the snare cable up and tight around the foot once the thrower trigger is tripped), an 8mm stainless swivel, and another 10 feet of aircraft cable to anchor the snare.

The whole time Vince had been using these snares, he had never lost an animal once it had tripped the snare's trigger. Now he just had to go out and set these snares to add to the four snares he already had set. *Vince Donnelly, trapper extraordinaire*, he thought to himself.

Vince threw the new snares in his hunting pack. He then put the pack, along with his cased Remington .308 rifle, in the toolbox of his 2003 Chevy Silverado and headed out.

Vince didn't know his boss very well, even though they played high school basketball against each other, but he seemed like a good, solid guy. Vince knew this job wasn't going to be something he could do long-term, but it paid the bills until something else came up.

Today, he was out checking his traps and setting a few more. From his home in Wauconda, WA, he headed north on Toroda Creek Road. Having spent most of his adult life in the area, Vince knew it like the back of his hand. As he was driving along, he thought about "the rule of the six B's" his boss had told him: "No booze, bud, babes, butts, brass, or brag." The rule about booze and bud (weed) was normal for nearly every job in the world. It was the other four that he didn't expect, but it all made sense. What they were doing was illegal as hell, and nobody wanted to go to jail, so the boss was extra careful. Babes, wives, or girlfriends are never to be involved. Cigarette butts have DNA on them and should never be left behind. Brass from fired ammunition is kind of the same as cigarette butts—never leave them behind. Bragging and women, the boss explained, are the two things that put more people in prison than anything else. Vince's boss always said that he lives by the Hells Angels motto of: "Three can keep a secret if two are dead."

After traveling about 15 miles, he took a logging road to the east into a spiderweb of Forest Service roads. This was where Vince felt most at home. Before he set the new snares, he needed to check the ones he already had out. At the first snare, there had been some activity because the bait had been dragged around, but somehow it just never worked out, and the snare had not been touched. Vince moved the bait back to where he wanted it and then worked on the "funnel," getting it just as he wanted.

Vince had been shown over and over how to set the snares, and it basically boiled down to two different set-ups. The first way was to place a bait in a spot where it was only accessible from one direction (against a large tree or a rock bank) and then stacking logs and rocks to form a V-shaped funnel, which narrowed the closer the animal got to the bait. This would leave the animal no choice but to step on the hidden snare trigger. The other method was to dig a hole about three feet deep and then set a bait in the bottom of the hole with the set snare on top. When the critter reached for the bait, the snare's trigger would be tripped, and the snare would be thrown up around its lower front leg above the foot.

Vince made it back to the truck and headed up the road for four more miles. He parked just beyond a sharp bend in the road and headed down the game trail to his next snare. Even before he could see it, he could hear the animal fighting the cable, which now had it tethered to a tree. Vince slowly and carefully made his way down toward the snare.

"Holy shit," Vince blurted out as he looked down at the very angry animal. *It's huge. If he could reach me right now, he would tear my head off*, Vince thought.

Vince quickly retreated to his truck, where he removed his rifle from the case. Vince knew he would only need one round, but because of its size, he loaded his rifle with four.

Back at the snare site, Vince was a little nervous about this. In all of his time in the woods, he had never seen a black bear this big before. Vince wanted to shoot it in the head, but it just wouldn't sit still, so he opted for the heart/lung shot, careful not to hit too far back on the animal. As the rifle barked in his hands, the bear went berserk. It was snarling and roaring so loud, he thought he could have heard it up by his truck a mile and a half back up the trail. His second round was placed in the bear's neck, which did the job, but because of its size, Vince wanted to take no chances, so he fired another round, this time to the head.

Now came the easy part. First, Vince searched the area he had been standing when he shot and recovered the two spent casings from the ground, adding them to the third casing he had just removed from the rifle's breech. Next, he released the snare from the bear's right-front leg, wrapping up the cable and placing the snare in his hunting pack. Then out came his knife, a 12" length of paracord, and a zip-lock baggie.

Vince carefully cut open the bear's body cavity, where he searched around for the liver. Upon finding the liver and making sure he didn't damage the gallbladder (attached to the liver), he cut out the liver with the attached gallbladder, laying it on top of the bear's carcass. Vince then carefully manipulated the gall to a position where he could tie the paracord around the neck of the gall, thus preventing the bile from leaking out. He then cut the gall neck (the tube at the top

71

of the gall) and carefully cut away the connective tissue between the gall and the liver. Five minutes later, he was holding an enormous gallbladder, which after admiring, he slipped into the baggie and gently placed in his hunting pack.

Vince then removed a water bottle and some paper towels, which he used to clean his arms, hands, and knife thoroughly. Explaining why you are covered in blood when there is no open hunting season might be a little tough to explain. The towels and empty water bottle went in a plastic garbage bag and back into his pack, leaving nothing behind. Vince then broke down his trapping set by removing the log and rock funnel, filling in the hole, and throwing leaves and sticks all around the site. Before he left, he took one last look around. All clean and all good. Even if someone found the bear, they would have no clue who had done it.

Back in his truck, he removed the gall from his pack just to admire it again. He was paid a flat $1.25 per gram on the gall, and this one had to be well over 300 grams. Not a bad day at the office, and he was only half done.

The next two snares were blanks. Vince decided he would give them each a couple more days before moving them.

After checking his snares, it was time to set more. Vince had already baited the sites (which were located miles apart) and had bear activity in all but one. Vince didn't like carrying a loaded rifle around in the woods this time of year because it would be pretty obvious he was up to no good, but walking into an active bear bait was always dangerous.

72

At his first new site, the deer he had killed five days ago was still there but had been chewed on. He dragged the deer carcass up against a huge tree and began to build a funnel to it. At the narrow end of the funnel, he dug a hole and placed the snare in place. Once it was set, he carefully covered the entire snare and wire with leaves and loose dirt. It was set, so Vince packed up and headed to the next site—a process he repeated until he had ten total snares set out.

Since baiting bear is illegal in Washington, Vince's boss had told him to use "Nature's bait" rather than the traditional bear baits such as doughnuts, pastries, or bacon grease. The boss explained that using nature's baits was cheaper, easier (no carrying buckets of bait through the woods), and was less obvious to anyone who came across it.

I'm doing better than the guys with dogs, Vince thought to himself. Even though he had never met one, Vince knew there were several other "employees" doing the same job. The boss didn't care how they went about our jobs, just as long as they followed his rules and kept their mouths shut. He had told Vince some guys were using hounds, some were trapping, and others were stand hunting (sitting in one place watching to see what came into a bait). All employees were told that if they were caught, they were to keep their mouths shut and take it like a man. The boss said he would pay the fines of anyone who got caught but couldn't do much about any jail the employee might be sentenced to. There was to be no snitching—period.

When Vince got home, he couldn't wait to weigh the gall. He dug around in the kitchen drawers until he found his wife's electronic food scale. When he plopped the huge gall on the scale, he couldn't believe his luck when he saw the scale read 413 grams. Using the calculator

73

on his phone, he calculated that he would get $516.25 for a day's work. Logging normally paid $200 to $250 a day, so this gig wasn't too bad.

CHAPTER 11

The gallbladder is a small, pear-shaped organ attached to the liver. The gallbladder of a bear ranges from the size of a walnut to the size of a large grapefruit (500+ grams) and is full of liquid bile. There are only two ways to obtain the bile from a bear's gallbladder: by cutting the gall out of a dead bear or by inserting a tube into the gallbladder of a live bear and draining it out (bear bile farming—a whole other story).

Records indicate bear bile has been used in traditional Chinese medicine since as early as 700 A.D. Bear bile is used in the treatment of everything from hyperlipidemia, intestinal, liver, and gallbladder illnesses to cancers, skin rashes, burns, and fevers. Contrary to popular belief, bear bile is not used as an aphrodisiac (which seems to be an American urban myth).

According to many modern scientists, the bile from bear gallbladder does indeed have some valid medical value. However, in 1995 Japanese scientists succeeded in chemically synthesizing bear bile. Today the active ingredient, Ursodeoxycholic Acid (UDCA), is made synthetically from cow bile (marketed in the U.S. under the brand name "Actigall"), thus eliminating the need for the gallbladder bile from bears. It was estimated in 2008 that 220,000 pounds of synthetic UDCA was already being used each year in China, Japan, and South Korea.

Despite the fact the very same active ingredients from bear gallbladder are now available at the pharmacy, many in the Asian culture believe only bile from bear gallbladder offers the healing powers sought.

75

Once the gallbladder has been removed from a dead bear (which can be done in less than five minutes by a skilled poacher), the "neck" of the gallbladder is tied off with a string to prevent the bile from escaping. At this point, the gallbladder has the consistency of a water balloon with the shape of a pear. The bladder is then hung to air dry, eventually leaving what appears to be a shriveled up, dried fig. The dried bile is powdered and mixed into sake, whiskey, teas, wines, and tonics. Bear bile can also be found in products such as pills, capsules, ointments, eye drops, shampoos, and throat lozenges.

In today's black market, buyers in the U.S. will pay between $100 and $600 for a single gall, but when they get to Asia, they sell for well over $4,000 each, making them far more valuable than gold.

CHAPTER 12

Clay and Lisa pulled up to Moe's gate at about four p.m. and found it closed, but Clay knew Moe always insisted the gate remain closed, even when someone was home. As Moe once explained to Clay, "If you only close the gate when nobody is home, it makes it pretty easy for burglars to tell if anyone is home by just driving by."

Clay punched in the code and then led Lisa up the hill to the shop. As Clay showed Lisa where to park, Garma came out to greet them.

"How are my favorite two game wardens today?" she asked with a radiant smile.

"I'm totally awesome as normal," Clay responded as he gave her a big hug. "Where are the monsters?"

"Shenden is at a friend's house, and Chesa is helping her dad at the store, but they both know you are coming over Sunday and can't wait to beat you at cornhole again," Garma said with a smile.

"Yeah, well, warn them. I've been practicing, and they are going down this time," Clay answered.

Garma then turned her attention to Lisa. "We're all so excited you and Emily will be here too. I hope you all like kabobs. Any other requests?"

"Kabobs will be perfect. Is there anything we can bring?" Lisa asked.

77

"Absolutely not. We are honored to have you in our home and to share a meal. Just bring hunger. We will take care of the rest," Garma answered. "Clay tells me you have a dog."

"Yes, we do. Her name is Mayhem. We just call her May. She's a three-year-old Irish Setter. She's a bit of a bonehead, and she has a ton of energy, but overall she's a wonderful dog," Lisa said.

"Please bring her along. Maybe she can wear the girls out," Garma said with a chuckle.

After another round of hugs, Lisa jumped in Clay's truck for the ride home. "So, what's with the security gate?" Lisa asked Clay.

"I'm pretty sure I told you about this, but two years ago, a guy came into the Moe-Mart stumbling drunk. Anyway, this dickhead came in to get a roll of freezer paper and felt the need to brag to Moe about the deer he had shot that morning, even showing him a photo on his phone. The only problem was, the season had been closed by about two months," Clay explained. "Well, the minute the guy left his store, Moe called me and gave me the guy's license number and even texted me a photo of the clown getting into his truck. Next thing you know, the guy was sitting in jail, wondering how the game warden knew about his deer."

Clay continued, "It wasn't too long before three of the windows in Moe-Mart were shot, and the side of his store was painted with 'Go home raghead.' It scared him, and I don't blame him. We never could prove it was the poacher, but it had to be. That's when Moe beefed up his security."

78

"Can't say I blame him," Lisa said.

"Moe has guts, and you should see him when he's fired up. I sure as hell wouldn't want to fight him. He's in awesome shape, and I think he's like a tenth-degree black belt or something. For a short little guy, he's pretty damned tough. Guess he had to be, to be a cop in Myanmar," Clay explained.

"Glad he's on our side then," Lisa noted.

"You want to go put up some cameras tomorrow morning?" Clay asked.

"Sure. You want me to pick you up around 7:00, then?"

"Works for me. Let's go plainclothes in our new truck to be stealthy," Clay said.

Clay dropped Lisa off at her home and then headed home himself, where he signed "out-of-service" with the state patrol dispatch (as required). He grabbed a beer and his department laptop, settled into his command center, and opened his department email.

"Looks like we have a bigger problem than we thought," was the subject line of the email from Sean. The email was addressed to Clay, Lisa, and cc'd to Captain Owen from Region 2.

> I sent out Lisa's request for information to all supervisors in the eastside regions and, so far, have heard back from four different sergeants. It looks like this poaching spree is not unique to our area. They are still working on getting me numbers, but it looks like those four

sergeants came up with somewhere around forty-five animals shot and left during the same period.

As you can guess, nobody had any reason to think this was more than a local problem in their particular area. I have asked everyone to send me what reports they have, as well as lists of evidence recovered and any suspects. I gave them until Monday to get that information to me. Once I hear back from everyone, I might suggest a meeting or at least a conference call between all the detachments affected. That area just north of Spokane seems to have been hit the worst since they account for nine of the kills. One other difference is several of them said the gallbladders had been removed from the bears they found.

You two might think I'm nuts, but what about B.C.? Quite a bit of this stuff seems to be happening close to the US/Canada border, so I was wondering if maybe it was also occurring there. I can reach out to the B.C. Conservation Officer Service, if you would like, and pick their brains too. Let me know what else I can do to help. Sean

The very next email was from Lisa in reply to Sean's message.

Wow, this makes a tough problem much tougher. Now we don't know where this is all centered or if it all is really connected or not. In my opinion, I think asking the B.C. officers for information sure can't hurt any. As for a meeting or conference call, it kinda sounds like too many officers for a conference call, so how about a meeting at a central location? Thanks for the help, Sean. Lisa

Clay added his two cents' worth in his reply.

I also agree with contacting B.C. As for a meeting vs. conference call, I would like to decide once we hear back from everyone. Scheduling a conference call will always be easier than picking a day where everyone can take the time to drive to one spot. This coming week, Lisa and I are meeting with both of the local Forest Service officers and the Sheriff's office. Lisa already briefed all four of the local troopers. We are heading up tomorrow (Friday) morning to put our cameras up. We will keep you posted. Clay.

Clay sat back in his chair and silently thought through this. Hypothetically, if these were all connected (or at least the majority of them were connected), then it has to be coordinated by one or two people who are calling the shots. If they are stripping the gallbladder from the bears, where are the gall going? Also, if this is all about bear gall, why kill the deer and elk?

CHAPTER 13

David Byrd lived on one of the largest Indian reservations in the state of Washington. The two-million-acre reservation was home to around 8,000 people, as well as a very healthy and diverse wildlife population. Mule deer, white-tailed deer, elk, moose, bears, eagles, and cougars all thrive on the reservation in healthy numbers. Unfortunately, like with off-reservation land, the tribe's wildlife was impacted by a few bad apples, and Byrd was one of the worst. Byrd hunted everything that moved—his motto being, "If it's brown, it's down, and if it flies, it dies."

In addition to his total disregard for both state and tribal wildlife laws, Byrd also contributed to the tribe's growing drug problem. Byrd brought both heroin and meth onto the reservation and had no hesitancy at all in spreading his poison among his own people. Anything for money.

On this particular day, David wasn't going after game. As a matter of fact, he didn't even have a firearm. On this day, Byrd was simply making an off-reservation re-up run. Today he was picking up his monthly replenishment of dope—both meth and heroin. He was stocking up with two ounces of meth and a quarter pound of H, which would normally satisfy his customer's needs for the month.

From his house, it was exactly forty-three miles to Republic, where he was supposed to meet his supplier. David always looked forward to delivery day because as soon as he got back home, he was gonna get laid by every hot chick around. A fresh re-supply brought in the babes, and he was just the man to satisfy them all.

82

David had been in the "distribution business" (as he called it) since middle school. He started with weed, but now that it was legal in Washington, his weed sales had gone to hell. Sometimes what separates a successful business from a failed business is adaptability. David was able to switch to the more profitable meth trade by his sophomore year in high school. With a strong customer base in meth, he expanded further to include heroin. In recent years he sold at least twice as much heroin as meth, not because meth users switched, but because more "non-users" of hard drugs had become heroin users, thanks to their doctors. Doctors, with their generous prescriptions for pain meds, helped David's sales skyrocket. His business tripled to the point he was now moving $15,000 to $18,000 of dope a month, much of which was free and clear profit for him.

About an hour after leaving home, David saw the road where the meet was supposed to occur. The meet was scheduled to be at 11:00, and it was already 10:52. David knew his supplier wasn't very patient. Taking a right on Adams Road, David continued about a mile before pulling alongside the 2017 white Dodge Ram 1500. When he saw someone sitting in the passenger seat, Byrd almost kept going. "So much for always coming alone," he muttered to himself. After a couple of seconds of thought, David decided to at least talk to Amy to see what the hell was going on.

"Hey, girlfriend, who's your buddy?" David questioned.

"Well, you have been a very reliable partner, and we decided it was time for you to meet your boss," Amy answered. "David, this is Mike. Mike, this is David."

83

David's anxiety level was climbing just thinking of meeting the main man, especially on a day he was almost late. Since the day David got in with these guys, he had always been warned about "the big guy." There were stories of how slow and painful he could make the death of anyone who crossed him. He was not one to be jerked around.

"Glad to meet you," David said, not knowing how to address him. The "main man" was a scary dude. Although he was an average-sized white guy, his black eyes and intimidating glare gave him the appearance of an axe murderer. Now David fully understood why nobody wanted to screw with this guy.

"I hear you are one of our top-selling distributors, and I just wanted to finally meet you. Is Amy treating you right?" asked Mike.

"No complaints from me. The product is always good. Amy is always on-time, even when I'm not, and the payment plan works great for me."

"Speaking of which, you got something for me?" Amy asked.

"I do," David answered as he reached into the console box next to him on the front seat. He handed Amy a package wrapped in a brown paper bag. "Check it if you want, but it's all there."

"I'm sure it is," Amy said in return as she handed him a similar bag.

"Well, it was nice to finally meet you, David. I look forward to many years of successful business together. Just remember the six B's, and you'll be fine. I think you understand," Mike said as Amy started the engine. "Take care, buddy," he called out, and then they were gone.

"Holy shit!" David exclaimed to an empty truck. As he reached for the ignition key, he noticed how badly his hands shook. "That's one bad-ass dude." Byrd got a small glass vial out from his pants pocket, tapped a little brown onto the back of his hand, and snorted it all at once. He had to calm his nerves for the drive back.

David made it about fifteen minutes down the road when he realized he was still pretty stressed and needed another bump. Once again, he took out the vial and poured a small hit on the back of his hand, but this time, he was steering with his knees at 60 mph while he did so.

Byrd felt the pickup tip hard to the right as it wandered into the ditch on the right side of the road. He felt the sudden jerk of the steering wheel as the right front tire dug into the soft dirt/gravel mix of the borrow ditch. Byrd never felt the impact of his Toyota Tacoma pickup truck slamming into the trees at over 50 mph.

Coming to rest on the driver's side, with the right rear wheel still spinning, the truck was demolished. As gasoline and oil leaked onto the ground, so did a good deal of David's blood. David Byrd was now a cop's dream—under the influence, suspended driver's license, unable to run or fight, lying motionless against the driver's door, with an open paper bag full of narcotics sitting on top of him. It was almost comical.

Trooper Clint Greer was the first to arrive at the scene. He called in his location, put on the required campaign hat, and then rushed up to

85

the truck, which he fully expected to find empty. Looking down into the cab through the passenger side window, Clint first thought the driver was deceased, but he then noticed bubbles of blood coming from the corner of Byrd's mouth as he exhaled. "1273 Omak, I have a one-car single-occupant rollover with injuries. Request fire, aid, and assistance," Trooper Greer calmly announced. Once Greer was certain help was on the way, he ran to his car, where he retrieved a wool blanket from the trunk. Back at the truck, he leaned in the open passenger-side window and gently spread the blanket over Byrd's face. Greer then moved around to the shattered windshield. Without some help, the windshield was the only way to access the driver safely. Using his ASP collapsible baton, Trooper Greer began the process of removing the front windshield.

Once the windshield was removed, Greer replaced his leather gloves with a latex pair. He then lifted the blanket from Byrd's head as the shards of glass fell away from him. Shoving the airbags out of the way, Trooper Greer reached for Byrd's neck, where he felt a faint but steady pulse. He thought about the situation for a few minutes and came to the conclusion he would likely do more harm trying to move the driver than to leave him the way he was until help arrived. In an effort to make the driver more comfortable, Greer moved all of the debris off him, including the paper bag. When Greer picked the paper bag up by one corner, he could clearly see the zip-lock baggies full of narcotics in the now open paper bag—along with a cell phone. The trooper photographed the items of evidence and placed them to the side where he could keep an eye on them while still attending to the driver.

"1273 Omak, requesting a supervisor to the scene," Greer advised dispatch.

Within the hour, Byrd was on his way to the Omak General Hospital, and his truck was on its way to impound. Fifty-nine grams of crystal meth, 116 grams of brown heroin, and a $40 LG Rebel FlashFone cell phone were secured in evidence bags, and the troopers were wrapping up the accident investigation.

Byrd remained unconscious for the entire ambulance ride and had no idea his life would be over one way or the other by the end of the day. The emergency room doctor did a quick visual examination of David as he woke from his nap. Upon awaking, Byrd's first thought was relief that he had not been killed, but the joy of that discovery immediately faded when he noticed his right wrist was handcuffed to the bed rail. David was administered a mild sedative and ordered to be sent to imaging to see what problems existed internally.

For all the blood David had lost, he didn't have much serious damage to his body. His complete list of injuries included several broken bones in his left hand, a broken nose, a hairline skull fracture, a severe concussion, a large cut to the head, and a shattered right ankle— overall, not too bad considering.

Mr. Byrd's bigger problem came walking through the emergency room door with a warrant in hand for a blood draw. No matter how much Byrd objected, his blood was drawn and his fate sealed. With two prior DUI convictions and a stint in prison for possession of methamphetamines, Byrd wasn't feeling very confident about his future. With his left hand and wrist in a cast, there was only the right wrist that could be handcuffed. At least the trooper had been thoughtful enough to link three sets of handcuffs together, so he could reach far enough to eat and sign documents.

Byrd thought about his shitty luck. He hadn't had a traffic accident in his 20 years of driving, even when he had been drunk on his ass. But now, he just had to go and wreck his truck off-reservation with more than a quarter of a pound of narcotics sitting on his lap. He was screwed; Johnnie Cochran couldn't have gotten him out of this mess.

CHAPTER 14

Clay was down, 17 to 8, when Lisa, Emily, and Mayhem arrived. Over the objections of eleven-year-old Chesa, who wanted to finish Clay off, the cornhole game was put on hold while everyone greeted the guests.

Lisa exited the car with a huge bouquet of flowers, which she presented to Garma.

With a hug, Garma said, "I thought I told you not to bring anything. But they are beautiful. Thank you."

"They are from our garden," Emily added. "It's the first garden we have ever had."

While Garma gave the ladies a tour of the house and grounds, Chesa and Shenden started up a game of "keep away" with Mayhem.

"You ready for another one?" Moe asked as he reached in the beer frig of his outdoor kitchen.

"Just so you won't be drinking alone again—sure," Clay responded.

"We're far outnumbered, my friend," Moe said as he spread his arms wide with a feigned look of concern. "Four women, two girls, and a female dog. Not good."

"I'm thinking we will survive," Clay said with a grin.

"You get all of your cameras put up?" Moe asked Clay.

89

"Yeah, Lisa and I put up six on Friday morning, so in total, we have seven out now," Clay answered.

"That covers a lot of ground, but it's still a shot in the dark." Clay went on. "I figure that if we see the same vehicle coming up the same road multiple times, and at weird hours, that at least would give us someone to look at. Right now, we are just spinning our wheels."

As Lisa joined the conversation, Moe said, "How about employing the Myanmar Motion Sensor?"

"The what?" Lisa asked.

"The Myanmar Motion Sensor," Clay answered. "It's the poor man's version of a remote motion sensor that Moe showed me years ago."

"In Myanmar, we didn't have much money for electronics, so we had to improvise. For us to monitor forest roads, in order to know which roads were being used in a certain timeframe, we used the Myanmar Motion Sensor. The highly sophisticated sensor can be made from sticks," Moe explained. "To employ this technique, you will first need to find a four to five-foot stick about a half-inch diameter. You then break the stick in half and gently place it across at least one of the road's tire ruts and push the broken ends back together so it looks like it has never been broken. When someone drives over the stick, it snaps back into two separate pieces or more, so you can easily tell if someone has been up that particular road since the time you set up the Myanmar Sensor."

"Simple, inexpensive, safe, and effective," Moe said using his best television pitchman voice. "Nine out of ten game wardens worldwide swear by the Myanmar Motion Sensor. But what would you expect to pay? $49.99, $39.99, $29.99? No, it's just $19.99, and if you call now, we will even throw in a second Myanmar Motion Sensor for free. Call now. Operators are standing by. Call us collect, call us direct, but call us today."

"I have used the stick trick dozens of times. It's better than nothing. If the stick is broken and it's on a dead-end road, you know it's worth checking out to see why someone went up there. If the stick gets broken on a regular basis, then it's time for a covert camera," Clay told Lisa.

"So, what's the deal on your new truck?" Moe asked as he pointed at the unmarked F-150.

"Our investigative unit loaned it to us for the spree kill case. We figured we would save it for when we do need to be a bit stealthy, like driving by a suspect's house to check things out," Clay answered.

"You want to leave it in the shop? I have plenty of room, and that way, nobody would ever see it parked here at all," Moe asked.

"Sure, if you don't mind," Lisa answered.

"Let's move it in there while we are thinking about it," Moe responded.

Moe punched in the code on the keypad, and the main door lifted open, revealing a huge shop with every tool known to man, a Cub

91

Cadet riding mower, and a beautiful 18' Hewescraft Pro V with a 150hp Mercury outboard. Lisa only really noticed the boat.

"Same code as the gate," Moe said.

"Nice boat. It looks brand new," Lisa said to Moe.

"As Clay can tell you, when we first moved here, I was out on the lake all the time. As a matter of fact, the first time we met was on the lake when Clay checked me. Hell, just about every time I went fishing, I saw Clay. Finally, I told him if he was going to keep stalking me like that, he might as well jump in and join me. This summer, I have only had it out once," Moe answered.

"Moe decided he didn't like relaxing in a nice comfortable boat. He now prefers to run around in waders, beating the water to a froth with a fly rod," Clay interjected.

"Ignore him. Do you like to fish?" Moe asked Lisa.

"I love fishing, and so does Emily."

"Let me know when you both have the same day off, and we will take it out, just as long as you promise not to violate international law, like someone else I know," Moe chuckled.

"Sounds like a story I've got to hear," Lisa said.

"Two years ago, Clay and I went out on Lake Osoyoos in pursuit of the ever so elusive kokanee. We were trolling along, picking up a fish now and then, when your partner here finally realized we had trolled into the Canadian end of the lake. We both had Canadian fishing licenses, so that wasn't a problem. And as you know, as long

92

as you don't touch land or make contact with another boat, you can boat into Canada and back without clearing customs. But the thing Canada does frown on is bringing a pistol into their country. Well, once our genius here woke up enough to finally realize where we were, he freaked. It seems he had decided he needed to bring a pistol fishing, which I didn't know because he never told me. He insisted I turn back south immediately. He was so wound up, I thought he was going to call Canadian Customs and turn himself in. It was priceless seeing him sweat like that," Moe said with a wide smile.

"I only wish I had been there," Lisa said

Once the truck was backed in the shop and the shop was locked, Moe asked Clay and Lisa, "Is there anything more I can do to help?"

"Not unless you have an extra half-dozen covert cameras sitting around," Lisa answered.

"I don't, but have you ever seen the Striker remote sensors?" Moe asked.

"I've never heard of them."

"They are battery-powered remote sensors that are tripped by large metal objects," Moe said. "I guess they must use a magnet or something to detect not motion but metal, so they won't trip when a moose walks by. But when a vehicle goes by, they send you a text message. They are pretty incredible."

"That would be awesome to have. I don't even know if SIU knows about these," Lisa responded.

93

"I would be willing to bet you could borrow one or two from some of your federal counterparts. I'm sure most of the federal law enforcement agencies employ them," Moe added.

"You are so helpful. I just want to let you know how much Clay and I both appreciate your help. Even if Clay would never tell you so," Lisa said.

"Look, I can honestly say I'm not doing this just for you two. More animals poached means less for the legal hunters, and legal hunters mean tourist dollars for my business," Moe explained. "If this small gesture helps catch the guys doing this, I will be thrilled. After dinner, I will show you the website for the Striker sensors."

"Well, thank you, Moe. We do appreciate it," Clay said. "Now on to another subject. Have you met the new taxidermist?"

"Matt? Yeah, I see him about twice a day since his shop is right down the road from my store. He comes in every morning and gets a cup of coffee and something from our vast selection of deep-fried and microwaved gourmet breakfast items," Moe answered. "Why? Do you think he's involved somehow?"

Lisa answered, "We don't have any reason to suspect him at all, except for the timing of his arrival, the fact he's in a commercial wildlife business, and he looks like an outlaw biker. Plus, he gives me the creeps."

"I'm not sure any of that will move you any closer to probable cause of anything," Moe said with a smile. "Look, I'm not vouching for him or anything, but I talk to him damned near every day, and I don't get a sense of anything wrong. I think he just considers himself to be a modern-day mountain man or something, but I think he's harmless."

Mayhem was done. Her brain wanted to keep playing with the girls, but her body said stop, so she took her tennis ball to a shady spot on the lawn to lay down. The girls, on the other hand, still had some energy in reserve and came to grab Clay. They had a game to finish.

"Lisa, why don't I show you those sensors now while Clay gets his butt kicked by two little girls," Moe offered.

"Let's do it," Lisa said as she followed Moe into the house.

Moe's office was simply awe-inspiring. Steeped in cherry wood and leather, the furniture alone looked like something out of the White House Oval Office. From the Oxford diploma and the honors bequeathed upon him to the various photos displayed, it was amazing. The entire office gave off a sense of importance.

As Moe was firing up his computer, Lisa asked, "What was it like there?" while pointing at a photo of Moe standing in front of a formation of hundreds of well-armed police officers.

"I love the country and the people of Myanmar, but its government is out of control," Moe responded. "Like with many people in government service, if it weren't for the politics, I would have stayed. But in Myanmar, with the change in politics came the mass murder of tens of thousands of innocent people. Myanmar comprises fifty-three million people from ten different ethnic groups, many of whom will fight each other to the death. I personally survived two different assassination attempts, and I still would have stayed to try to effect some change had it not been for my family. It was time to go. A beautiful country with great people was being run by madmen. That pretty well sums it up. We will likely never be allowed to return, nor would it be safe to."

"Working law enforcement in Myanmar had one major advantage over how you work here," Moe said with authority. "In Myanmar, we killed our poachers and drug dealers. We found it significantly reduced the number of repeat offenders."

With a couple of mouse clicks on the computer, Lisa was looking at the Striker Surveillance Systems website.

"You're right. These would be perfect. I will let SIU know about these, and we will see if we can stir one or two up to borrow. Thanks," Lisa told Moe.

As they walked back outside, Lisa wondered if he had been kidding about that killing poachers thing, but she decided she didn't want to know.

The minute Lisa stepped outside onto the deck, the girls came running up to her, advising Lisa that Emily had volunteered her to help defeat the girls.

The stage was set for the Emily/Lisa team to go up against the team of Shenden/Chesa for the cornhole championship of the free world.

"I hope you're better than Clay," Chesa said straight-faced.

CHAPTER 15

In 1996, Initiative 655, a ban on hunting bears with the aid of bait or dogs, was passed by the voters. As a result of I-655, many hound-hunters sold their dogs and got out of the sport, while others, such as Gregg, kept on going as they always had. When Washington passed their new law, they left a huge loophole. While the law prohibited the use of dogs when hunting mountain lions, bobcats, lynx, and bears, it left open several other species, including raccoon and coyote. The less scrupulous hunters continued hunting cats and bears with hounds, but if asked, they were hunting raccoons or coyotes. Gregg was one such hunter.

Gregg left Walla Walla, heading toward Dayton at about 3:15 a.m. to beat the heat and to hopefully catch something before the normal people even climbed out of bed. As he turned off Hwy. 12 and onto the Jasper Mountain Road, Gregg wondered if he would have success or not. It had been three days since he caught the last one, and he was getting a bit concerned, but he was going to try a new spot this day. Four days prior, Gregg brought his 30-30 rifle up and dumped a couple of deer for bait. He hoped that by now, those carcasses were drawing in the bears.

Gregg, like the majority of houndsmen, drove a beat-up ten-year-old Toyota Tacoma. Gregg had properly outfitted the truck for the purpose of hunting with hounds. In the bed of his truck, Gregg had built a wooden dog box with six separate dog compartments. The top of the dog box was carpeted to keep the dogs from sliding and was surrounded on three sides—the back was open—with a railing about

20" high and eyebolts all the way around. The hood of his truck was also carpeted with a single eyebolt dead center in the middle of the hood.

When Gregg got to the intersection of the Canright Road and the Jasper Mountain Road, he pulled his Toyota off the road and cut the engine. He saw no lights and didn't hear a thing other than the light wind blowing through the ponderosa pines. Gregg opened one door at a time on the dog box, which took up the majority of his truck's bed. As each hound poked its head out of the box, Gregg activated the dog's shock collar with a magnet and then released the dogs so they could lighten their loads. After every one of his five hounds had pooped, he put four of them on the carpeted top of his box and clipped them to the railing's eyebolts, so they couldn't jump or fall off the box. The fifth dog, Griz, was the strike dog and had the honor of riding on the hood. The strike dog was simply the dog with the best nose. It is much easier for the dogs to sense the smell of the game they were trained to pursue from the top of the dog box rather than in it.

Just as the sun began to break over the horizon, Gregg pulled back onto the Jasper Mountain Road and began slowly creeping along, waiting for the dogs to sing. About halfway between the Canright Road and the Bundy Hollow Road, Gregg pulled in a dirt two-track road, which headed north, to one of the deer he had left for bait. Gregg had only made it a mile or so down the narrow dirt road when the dogs went crazy. Gregg stopped the truck and turned all five dogs loose, and they immediately took off at full speed. He put his hunting pack on, grabbed his 30-.30, and hustled after the dogs. The chase of a bear can go for hours, covering many miles, but this bear decided to take one of the first trees he came to in hopes of getting away from the snarling pack of hounds right behind him.

After traveling only about half a mile, Gregg got to the tree and saw five hounds all baying (barking and howling) up a tree as an average-sized 140-pound black bear sat staring down at the chaos from 30' up the tree. A well-placed 30-.30 bullet dropped the bear from the tree—almost on top of two of the dogs. The second the bear hit the ground, the dogs attacked. All five dogs were barking, biting, and pulling on the bear, an action houndsmen refer to as "worrying." After gathering up the dogs, Gregg walked them back to the truck, where they were rewarded and then put back into the box.

Gregg then returned to the bear, where he removed the gallbladder and all four paws in less than 15 minutes. After cleaning the blood off with paper towels and a bottle of water, Gregg placed the gall in a zip-lock bag, which he placed in an old Safeway bag, which then went into his pack alongside the paper towels and water bottle. About 50 yards from his truck, Gregg hid the pack in some brush and then walked the rest of the way to the truck, where he made sure he was alone before returning to retrieve the pack. Next, Gregg used the extendable hand-crank to lower his spare tire to the ground. After placing the Safeway bag full of goodies on top of the spare tire, he cranked it securely back in place.

Gregg sat on the tailgate of his truck and pulled out the $40 LG Rebel FlashFone cell phone he had been given, and left a voice message for the boss. "It's Gregg. I'm ready anytime now, so just let me know when and where."

On the trip home, Gregg got a call on his own personal phone. When he saw the call was coming from the Washington Department of Corrections, he muted it and let it go to voicemail. Gregg didn't even need to listen to the voicemail because he already knew what the message was. Once again, they were a few officers short on a shift at the penitentiary and needed him to cover a shift tonight if he was available.

Screw 'em. My time off is way more important than a few extra hours of OT. Besides, I can actually make more money hunting than working at the "pen," Gregg thought.

CHAPTER 16

Today was the meeting with the Forest Service LEOs (Law Enforcement Officers), all two of them. The two officers had agreed with Lisa to meet at their office in Omak. While Clay knew both officers fairly well, Lisa had only briefly met one and had not yet met the other.

The woman at the front counter obviously was told to expect them since she buzzed them in almost as soon as they had entered the lobby. Darlene, according to her nametag, directed them back to the LEO's office. Brent and Rick rose from their desks and introduced themselves to Lisa—mostly ignoring Clay. After the introductions were completed, the four entered a small conference room near the back of the building.

Lisa opened the conversation by showing them the map of the kill sites, which Clay had put together. "As you can see on that map, the majority of the animals killed were killed on Okanogan National Forest Service land, making this a problem for all of us," Lisa explained. "Have either of you seen anything that looks like it might be associated with these spree kills?"

"No, nothing like that at all," Officer Pendly said. "If we had, we would have called."

Clay jumped in, "We are in no way trying to pawn our work off on you guys. We're just asking you to keep your eyes peeled for anything at all that looks out of place or any vehicle you notice out and about way too much, rifle shots fired, dead critters, lights at night, any

101

of that stuff—please call us. Also, when you get a chance, grab us all of the license numbers you can from any vehicle you aren't sure about, especially any vehicles which are parked and empty."

"So, what's your best guess at this point—commercial poachers?" asked young Officer Stanton.

"We honestly have no idea at all. It could be a commercial operation, or it could be some crazed idiots on a long-term killing spree," Clay answered.

"Have you contacted U.S. Fish and Wildlife about this?" asked Officer Pendly.

"They are next on our list," Clay said as he wondered why he hadn't thought of that himself.

After another half-hour of conversation, Lisa and Clay walked across the Forest Service building's rear parking lot when Clay said, "I'm sure glad I thought about the U.S. Fish and Wildlife Service. I will give Super Special Agent Slader a call tonight. It's about time to catch up with him anyway. You haven't met him yet, have you?"

"No, but now that you came up with the brilliant idea of calling the feds, I guess I will be meeting him soon," Lisa sarcastically responded.

"You wanna go see the Sheriff now and fill him in?" Lisa asked.

"Why not." Clay replied.

Sheriff Kevin Bryant and Clay had known each other for a very long time. When Clay first moved to the county, Bryant was a brand-new deputy trying to figure the job out. The two men worked together often and made some damned good cases together. Although they didn't see each other that much anymore, their friendship was still intact.

While Clay could never understand how anyone would want a job that they had to campaign for, he knew the deputies stood behind their sheriff one hundred percent. Kevin turned out to be a great leader. He never asked his deputies to do anything he wouldn't be willing to do himself. He was honest to a fault and believed that treating his employees with dignity and respect was paramount to an efficient operation. Firm, fair, and consistent was his motto.

At 6'04" and 270 pounds, Sheriff Bryant was an intimidating man, even with the spare tire he wore around his waist.

"What can I do for you two troublemakers?" Sheriff Bryant said as he rose to greet his guests. After a handshake for Clay and a hug for Lisa, the two sat.

"I guess you already know we have had a hell of a poaching streak going on for a year now. We have found almost forty dead and wasted big game animals between the two of us, and we are no closer to a suspect than we were a year ago," Clay said.

"So, what can we do to help?"

"Please just get the word out to your deputies to keep their eyes peeled for anything suspicious and, most importantly, grab the license plates off any vehicles they find empty in the woods. These guys aren't generally road hunters. Their kills are normally at least a half-mile from any road, so they are either getting dropped off by someone, or they are parking their trucks somewhere while they do their thing. So, an empty truck in the woods is a red flag," Clay responded.

"Okay, that won't be a problem. What else have you got?"

"We would like them to call us anytime your deputies come across a suspect transporting a hunting rifle around—when it just doesn't fit. Anytime they find any animal parts, hair, or even blood during a contact, any rifle casings laying on the road, or any of that, we would appreciate a call," Lisa added.

"You've got it. I will put out a memo today asking for everyone to be extra vigilant in trying to get you some information," the Sheriff replied.

"I do have one request for you two. Our county is being poisoned by some asshole spreading around heroin laced with fentanyl. This has got to stop, so take a hard look at any doper you run across. Somebody knows where this is coming from, and I want to find that guy and lock his ass up."

"Will do," Clay answered as they stood to leave. "Thanks, old man."

"By the way, Lisa, don't quote me on this, but your wife is one kick-ass deputy. She has been tearing it up, and I'm not the only one who has noticed. If you ever try to get her to move anywhere else, you will have to deal with my ugly side," the Sheriff said with a wide smile.

"I didn't know there was anything but an ugly side of you," Clay said with a smirk.

"As they say here, we ain't going nowhere," Lisa answered.

Back in the patrol vehicle, Lisa asked, "About time to call the Federales, isn't it?"

"Yep, I guess it is," Clay said as he took out his cell phone.

"So you have never met Ryan Slader, huh?" Clay asked.

"Nope, not that I know of," Lisa answered.

"You wouldn't forget Mr. Personality," Clay said as he called Slader.

"Ryan, this is Clay Newberry over in Oroville. Hey, we have a major spree kill going on here, and I was wondering if you guys would be willing to give us a hand?" Clay asked.

After another ten minutes of explanation, Agent Slader answered, "Hey, I'm sorry, Clay, but that's just not the kind of case we deal with. After everything you have told me, I still don't see a federal nexus to this, and without that, we can't get involved. This sounds like it is totally a state problem. Sorry."

"Do you happen to have any Striker remote sensors?" Lisa said from the background.

"I'm not sure who that was, but the answer is no, I don't have any Strikers available right now. They are all out in the field."

"That was my partner, Lisa," Clay responded. "I guess we are on our own. I will call you back if we find a federal nexus. Thanks."

"Well, that was enlightening and helpful," Lisa declared.

"I absolutely hate the phrase federal nexus. That drives me nuts. Next time the feds ask for our help, I will tell them to call me back when they have a state nexus," said Clay. "I guess it's just you and me against the entire crime world."

"Who else would we need? We've got this," Lisa added, "but this does remind me. We need to get back to everyone who responded to our inquiry about similar poaching incidents around the state."

"Okay, while we are thinking about it, would you send Sean an email asking about where we are on that?" Clay asked.

"Will do," Lisa said as she began typing out the email.

"Well, now that we are done rubbing elbows with the muckety-mucks, how about we go check some cameras," suggested Clay. "We can swing by Moe's place, grab the unmarked truck, and go see what we have on camera."

"Fine with me, but I'm starving. Let's hit Miguel's first. If you are okay with Mexican today," Lisa suggested.

"Sounds good to me. It's my turn to buy."

Lisa and Clay were done with the chips and salsa appetizer and looking forward to their orders when their portable radios alerted them to a call for service. "Omak local wildlife patrols, a subject on the line reporting a poached bear, requesting a call-back."

106

After taking the reporting party's name and number, Clay volunteered to step outside to call the RP (reporting party).

"So, what's the deal?" Lisa asked as Clay slid back into the booth.

"An archery hunter was up Dead Horse Ridge, scouting for a place to put his tree stand for the upcoming archery deer season. He had walked out a well-used game trail until he came across a dead bear, which he says is fairly fresh," Clay said. "But here's the best part. He said the bear had been cut open, but all of the guts were still inside the bear. He said he thought maybe the poacher had been scared off before he could finish cutting up the bear, but you already know what I'm thinking."

"Missing its gallbladder?" Lisa asked.

"Yep, I hate to say it, but we've gotta get going. The RP is waiting for us so that he can lead us into the bear."

"Dead Horse huh? It just had to be in my area, didn't it?" Lisa said.

"Hey, you were just complaining nobody turns in poaching incidents to you. Be careful what you wish for."

Clay tried to settle up for the sodas and chips, but the restaurant said no charge because their meals weren't even prepared yet.

Forty minutes later, Clay and Lisa pulled in behind the RP's blue Ford F-250 and were immediately greeted by a younger clean-cut man dressed in camo. After introductions, the archery hunter led the two

107

wardens into the kill scene. Clay carried the metal detector while Lisa brought in the evidence kit.

The bear was only about 130 pounds and had only been dead for a day or two at most. As Lisa opened her evidence kit, Clay thanked the RP and told him he would get back to him as soon as they knew anything.

Clay began snapping photos while Lisa gloved up.

We appreciate the call on this, and we appreciate you taking the time to walk us in here," Lisa added.

"No problem. Good luck in finding the guy who did this. Hang him when you do find him. I hate to see people shoot things and just leave them. Gives all hunters a bad name," the RP said as he walked back toward his truck.

Lisa said goodbye to the RP as she shoved her hands into the bear's body cavity. After searching around for a minute or so, Lisa brought up the liver for Clay to see. "The gall is gone," she announced as she cut out a small tissue sample, hopefully for a future DNA comparison.

"Okay, so now let's see what they left behind," Clay answered as he began running the metal detector over the carcass, picking up a strong signal from just behind the bear's left-front shoulder.

The two wardens flipped the bear on its right side and began slowly and carefully cutting the hide away from the general area of the metal object picked up by the metal detector. After cutting an oversized hide patch out, the wardens could see the obvious "bloodshot" tissue trauma from the bullet. Lisa ran her gloved fingers through the tissue on the outside of the ribcage until she came out with the bullet. A subsequent pass with the metal detector showed no other bullets in the bear.

Lisa poured a little water on the bullet and then held it up for Clay to see.

"Perfect. That's the best bullet we have recovered so far," Clay said. "If or when we ever find who shot this bear, this bullet will be the nail in their coffin."

As Lisa finished up with the bullet, Clay began searching the surrounding area.

"Lisa, come here and take a look at this," Clay said as he was standing by a large red cedar tree.

When Lisa got to the tree, Clay pointed out the scuffs and marks in the tree's bark, about two feet up from the ground. "Something tore the hell out of this tree—all the way around."

"Looks like something was tied up here, like a cable or chain," Lisa responded.

"Good observation. It was a cable, and I will bet money that cable was attached to a bear snare on the other end. Take a look at the lower end of the front legs, would ya?"

"Yep, all the hair is missing right above the right-front paw," Lisa said.

109

"Okay, so what and where is the bait?" Clay asked as he began clearing the leaves, sticks, and needles away from the base of the cedar tree. "Okay, I now know what the bait was, but I still need to find it."

"So, what was the bait?" Lisa asked.

"Take a look at the dirt all around the tree. It's covered in deer hair," Clay responded. "The poacher tried to cover the scene with debris, but you can't get rid of that much deer hair."

The dead bear laid near a flat trail on a fairly steep, brushy hillside. Knowing most people take the path of least resistance, Lisa began looking for the deer in the brush below the trail.

"Got it. A small whitetail doe," Lisa told Clay.

Soon the two officers were processing the half-consumed deer, just as they had the bear, only the deer had suffered a through-and-through shot, so there would be no bullet to examine from this carcass.

On their hike back to the truck, Lisa said, "This scene didn't produce any evidence to help us locate the poachers, but it did tell us one thing we didn't know before."

"Yeah, it's confirmed. This is a commercial poaching operation, after all."

Lisa and Clay decided to return to the Mexican restaurant to finish where they left off before checking the cameras.

After their late lunch, Lisa and Clay drove separate trucks to Moe's, where they swapped vehicles before going out to retrieve photos from their covert cameras.

110

CHAPTER 17

Many decades ago, the clothier produced beautiful clothing for both men and women. He produced custom clothing exclusively for the wealthy elite in his home country, but with the downturn in their economy went his business. What was making him enough money for his family to live comfortably had dried to a trickle. The clothier had to find a new market for his designs, but everything he had tried lately had failed. As the world celebrated the end of the 20th century and the beginning of the 21st century, the clothier was making barely enough money to feed his family. The clothier had no other trade skills and began looking for labor jobs when one of his former clients, Phyu, came to him with a strange proposal.

Phyu asked the clothier to design and sew underclothing which was specifically designed to carry up to four kilograms of "sand' in a way such that nobody looking at the person wearing the specialized garments would know. The clothier knew it wasn't sand that would be carried, but he appreciated his client's attempt to ease his conscience. The money this client offered the clothier was much more than he had ever been paid for a garment before, and after all, he wasn't breaking any laws by making a garment specially designed to carry sand covertly.

The clothier tried multiple materials for the sand-suit, as he had dubbed it, from cotton to synthetics before deciding to stick with Lycra. Lycra is a form-fitting material that could stretch to six times its original size. The material is light, comfortable, and best of all, it forms to fit almost any body size or shape. The real challenge for the

111

clothier was how to make the Lycra hold the "sand" without moving around and pooling at the bottom of the suit.

After much experimentation, the clothier decided to make the garment so that it had a whole series of cloth tubes. These tubes would run the length of the clothing item and would be sewn about 1" wide, from top to bottom all the way around the garment, creating dozens of 1" cloth tubes. Loading the tubes presented another problem since the Lycra tubes remained shrunken tight when nothing was holding them open.

The solution to loading the tubes came to the clothier pretty quickly when he decided to attach a four-foot length of ¾" transparent PVC pipe to a large funnel. The clothier simply shoved the pipe to the bottom of each tube and then poured sand into the pipe through the funnel. Once the sand reached the top of the tube, the pipe was slowly pulled out, leaving the sand in the Lycra tubing. The last step was to sew the tube end closed.

The clothier then sewed together two layers of Lycra, creating the sand tubes by sewing them around a 1" PVC pipe, which, of course, was pulled out once the tube had been sewn. After the clothier completed his prototype smuggling garment, he loaded it with sand, put the Lycra undershirt on, and covered it with a button-up shirt.

Looking at his creation in the mirror gave the clothier a sense of accomplishment. He had just designed and created the perfect clothing for the discerning smuggler. As the clothier wore the loaded garment throughout the day, a problem arose; gravity was causing the sand to pool in the bottom of the tubes, making the bulges pretty obvious. The

112

solution was simple. Instead of making the tubes run vertically up and down the smuggler's body, he would make them run horizontally around the body. Four days after the clothier put together the first sand suit, he called his client to come in and see it. Before the client came in, the clothier loaded the sand suit with as much sand as he could fit in the suit, which came to 13 pounds or just over 6 kilograms, or 33% more weight than the suit was required to carry.

The client and an associate of his arrived at the clothier's shop in the late afternoon. The client was very anxious to see the garments, but the clothier first wanted to discuss what color material the client wanted, how many suits he wanted to be made, and the price to produce one. He told the client he could produce the suits for the equivalent of $350 U.S. dollars each. The client didn't seem at all interested in the materials or the cost, but he was very anxious to finally see the suit for himself.

"So, when do I get to see this suit?" the client asked.

"You have been looking at it for the 15 minutes you have been standing here," said the clothier as he opened his shirt to reveal the loaded undergarment. "Right now, this garment is loaded with over six kilos of sand."

"Absolutely amazing. You are truly a genius," said the client.

"I will make you a deal. I will pay $500 each, with a couple of conditions. First, you will not show these to anyone or talk to anyone about them. Second, you will not make these for anyone else, just me. Last, if anyone were to ask, you have never met me. Agreed?" the client added.

113

"Deal. So, how many do you want and when do you need them by?" asked the clothier.

"I will take six more just as fast as you can make them."

"Now that I have the prototype done, I can put one of these out every three days or so. I should be able to deliver six more to you in three weeks." the clothier answered.

"Perfect. I will await your call," the client said as he turned to leave. "Just remember our agreement."

CHAPTER 18

Leaving home with the load was never the problem; it was CBSA (Canada Border Services Agency) that was the real concern, but Naing was relaxed. At 71-years of age, Naing didn't exactly fit the profile of a drug smuggler, but in fact, she was carrying almost four kilos of heroin. Naing worried a lot more about her husband Cho, who carried a little more than three kilos of meth strapped to his body.

This was their fourth trip to Canada in two years, and they had never had a problem before. Twice her husband had to get out of his wheelchair so they could search it, but they never searched people's bodies upon arrival.

The key, they had been told, to successful body-smuggling is never to have a visible bulge from your cargo. The smuggler's clothes must look right and hang right, which is why both smugglers had been fitted with specially designed bodysuits. These bodysuits went on like a set of long underwear, covering the smuggler from their ankles to their chests, and could carry the load without making any visible difference in the smuggler's body shape.

Naing's personal touch to smuggling was to make herself such a pest that the customs officers couldn't wait to be done with her. As soon as she would enter the inbound customs area in Vancouver, B.C., she would make a beeline for the first customs officer she could find and would start asking questions and making demands on how to treat her wheelchair-bound husband. Nobody wants to spend time talking to an obnoxious 71-year old woman who won't stop making demands. They were normally through customs well ahead of the other passengers, and this day was no different. She could visibly see the stress drain from the customs officers when they were able to move Naing out of their area.

Once out of customs and in the main terminal, Naing called for their ride, "We are out of customs and on our way out of the terminal. We will see you in a few."

Maung answered, "Okay. I am in the silver Mercedes GLE again. See you soon."

Maung saw his aunt and uncle waiting on the curb in front of the baggage claim. Maung laughed as he noticed Uncle Cho was using the wheelchair again.

I've gotta give them credit, Maung thought. *They are good.*

After hugs all the way around, Maung helped Cho into the front passenger seat while Naing rolled the wheelchair prop to the rear of the car. Maung then folded the wheelchair and loaded it, with their baggage, in the back of the Mercedes.

"How's everything going here?" asked Cho.

"Couldn't be better. Since we switched to the drone, we haven't lost a single load," answered Maung.

"Excellent, but never let your guard down. The people here may be stupid, but even stupid people get lucky once in a while," Cho cautioned.

After the four-hour drive, they arrived at Maung's home, where they were greeted by the remainder of the family. Cho left the wheelchair in the car. He wouldn't need it until his return flight.

"I've gotta get out of these clothes. I'm baking in these," said Naing.

Naing and Cho settled into their room and immediately removed the bodysuits, placing them in plastic garbage bags to give to Maung.

Back downstairs, the couple enjoyed a victory drink while Maung took the suits to his shop. In the center of the small shop was a smooth-surfaced wooden door, covered with a layer of butcher paper, sitting across two sawhorses. Maung removed one of the four garments from the bag and laid it out on the table. When they first started using the bodysuits, Maung would take hours to carefully remove the stitching on the tube ends to recover the contents without damaging the suits so that they could be reused. After complaining about how it would take several valuable hours to remove the stitching without damaging the suits, the word came back to simply cut them open and then burn them. The suits were not worth the time and effort to recycle.

Once Maung had the first piece (the top Naing had been wearing) spread out, he suited up in a Tyvek suit, gloves, goggles, and a respirator.

Why in the hell do these people take this shit? Maung thought.

Maung ran his knife over the sharpening stones for a few strokes before testing its sharpness on a piece of paper. Then, with long strokes, Maung ran the knife down the length of each tube, spilling the contents onto the butcher paper. After running his fingers down each tube, spilling more of the contents onto the butcher paper, Maung threw the shredded top in another garbage bag. Next, Maung used a thin plastic sheet to scoop the brown heroin up and transfer it to zip-lock bags. Once he had scooped up as much as possible, he simply folded the butcher paper into a funnel shape and tapped the remaining dope into the baggies.

Maung repeated the process three more times until all of the cargo was safely tucked into baggies and ready for the next journey. As Maung was cleaning up, Cho walked into the shop.

"You want to see the drone, Uncle Cho?" Maung asked.

"Absolutely. As you remember, I was opposed to using these things, but you have proven how effective they have been."

Handing Cho a pair of latex gloves, Maung said, "As you taught us, we can't be too careful."

The drone was sitting on top of a large chest freezer in the rear of the shop. Cho was very interested in the machine, even picking it up to see the underside where the cargo pod sat.

How much will this machine carry in one load?" Cho asked.

"The Matrice will carry up to 13 pounds for 35 minutes and can fly totally autonomously," Maung explained.

"Excellent, and how many do you have now?"

118

"Two—one on each end of the route," Maung answered. "We are scheduled to send this one out to the Rainman at 4:45 tomorrow morning. Would you like to watch?"

"That would be excellent. Please wake me on time to see the launch," Cho answered, "but now it's time to eat."

Cho, Maung, and the other two men sat on the deck, drinking and smoking, while the women prepared the feast. Fresh vegetables were washed and cut, while the marinated meat was trimmed.

"Sweetheart, would you grab the shrimp out of the chest freezer?" Naing asked her niece.

"Sure, Auntie," Nu answered as she walked out the side door to the shop.

When Nu opened the shop door, she noticed the strange-looking helicopter thing sitting on top of the freezer, which she needed to get into. Not wanting to disturb the men, Nu gently moved the drone to the floor, so she could open the freezer to retrieve the prawns. Once she had the prawns out, she carefully returned the drone to its position on the freezer.

119

CHAPTER 19

One by one, Lisa drove to the cameras. Clay would quickly jump out and swap out the 32GB SanDisk SDHC memory card with an identical but empty card. Once in the truck, Clay would transfer the photos from the memory cards to a file on his laptop, wipe the card clean, and have it ready to swap out with the next card in the next camera—a process they followed for the next six cameras.

Once all seven cameras had been downloaded, Clay began surfing through the pictures as Lisa drove back to Moe's.

"Well, anything interesting?" asked Lisa.

"I'm only through the first two cameras so far, and nothing really to see. Altogether, in the five days we had them out, I would say about twenty vehicles went by each camera. Right now, I'm just looking for anything that jumps out at me or for any of my regular local poachers, but nothing," Clay answered. "I am going to load all of the photos onto this thumb drive, so we can both sit in the comfort of our homes and go through them one by one. I will make a list of all of the license numbers for each camera on a spreadsheet to see if there are any repeat vehicles."

"The only problem we have is there is no way to read the license plates of vehicles after dark. I can't even make out the make and model half the time."

"Well, look at you, tech-savvy all of the sudden. Sean better look out. You are sounding more like sergeant material."

"Hell, you never know. I might even get the lobotomy they require to make captain," Clay answered.

As the daylight was fading to an end, Clay and Lisa drove up to Moe's shop, where the whole clan came out to greet them. For the first time, the girls didn't run up and hug Clay but rather flew to Lisa like moths to a lightbulb.

"Looks like I've been replaced," Clay told Garma.

"All good things must come to an end, my friend," Moe said, "we can all be replaced."

After saying his goodbyes, Clay jumped into his truck and headed out. He smiled as he looked in his rearview mirror and saw the girls holding Lisa's hands as they tried their best to lead her away from her truck and toward their house.

Finally, at home, after a long day, Clay first sat down to dinner with Karen. They had a long-standing tradition of eating dinner at the table rather than in the family room, where they ate every other meal. Since their son, Brian, left for college three years ago, Clay had petitioned Karen to change the rules so that the family room would work for all meals, but the request was denied.

Once dinner was done and Karen and Clay had caught up with each other on the day's events, Clay took his state-issued laptop to the command center. He spent the next two and a half hours combing through the covert camera photos. Only the fourth camera, which had been set up on the Forest Service 2320 road, had captured anything of real interest. At 18:37 last Thursday, one of the local poachers by the

121

name of Eric Bradford passed by the camera on the way in. Then at 18:48, a silver Toyota Tacoma drove in right behind Bradford. Clay zoomed in on the silver Toyota and could clearly identify Matt Davis as the driver and sole occupant. Exactly twenty-two minutes later, Davis drove out and was followed by Bradford.

"What in the hell were they doing up there for twenty-two minutes?" Clay wondered.

Clay finished up on the photos and then entered the license numbers, vehicle descriptions, road names, times, and dates onto a spreadsheet, which he emailed to Lisa.

Clay then took out his cell phone and texted Lisa, "We've got a road up by Clear Lake, I want to take a careful look at in the morning. If you're up for it, swing by in the morning and grab me. No need for stealth mode for this. We can take a work truck."

"See you at 8:00?" Lisa responded.

"See you then," Clay confirmed.

After the text conversation with Lisa, Clay opened his department email. In addition to the twenty-plus worthless emails was one from their esteemed leader—addressed to both Clay and Lisa.

> I have now heard back from five different detachments in three regions. So, not including the animals killed within our boundaries, officers have located forty-nine kills which seem to fit the pattern we have up here. Of those forty-nine, forty-one were bears, and the remainder were all deer. I asked about missing gallbladders and learned that of the forty-one bears, thirty-six were missing the gallbladder

122

while the other five were undetermined due to scavenger activity. Following this email, I will send you the case reports I have received thus far (only four).

In these reports, two things jumped out at me. First, in speaking with the Sergeants and reading the case reports, nobody has any evidence of value other than bullets. None of the officers have any solid suspects. Secondly, all eight deer were found at or near the bear kill sites. I assume this sounds familiar to you two. I updated the Captain as well as the chief, and they obviously would like the see these guys brought to justice before they wipe out every bear in the state. I will leave scheduling a meeting, for all involved officers and supervisors, up to you two. Just keep me in the loop.

I'd like to keep you in the loop, Sean boy, and then I would like to throw the other end of the rope over a limb and lift you up, Clay thought.

Clay responded to the email.

Sean: Since it sounds like none of the other officers have any evidence that we don't, I'm not sure what good a meeting would do. I would suggest we just designate one person to gather any and all information in one spot so that it can be disseminated to all involved. Since you are already acting in that capacity, I would suggest you take care of that while Lisa and I do the legwork. Clay

CHAPTER 20

At 7:40, Karen yelled, "Clay, she's here."

Clay welcomed Lisa in while Karen got her a cup of coffee.

"Have you had breakfast yet?" Karen asked Lisa.

"No, but that's fine. I'm good," Lisa answered.

"How do you like your eggs?" Karen asked, refusing to take no for an answer.

"By the dozen," Clay butted in. "The woman can eat half of her body weight in one sitting."

"Clay, that's not nice to say," Karen said.

"But accurate," Clay answered.

"Over easy would be fine. But you don't have to."

While breakfast was on the stove, Lisa asked Clay, "So what did you see on the Clear Lake camera?"

"Do you know who Eric Bradford is?" Clay asked.

"Doesn't ring a bell."

"Bradford is a piece of human garbage who lives down your way. Three years ago, I pinched him for bear-baiting down by Loomis. A year before that, I got him for exceeding the limit on deer. He's a total rat. Always heard he's a big doper too," Clay went on. "Around 6:30

124

last Thursday night, Bradford drove in on the 2320 road, and about ten minutes later, guess who drove in right behind him?"

"I give up."

"The new taxidermist, Matt Davis," Clay replied. "They were in there exactly twenty-two minutes before they both drove out."

"That's really strange," Lisa said. "Definitely worth checking out. Got any guess as to what they were doing up there?"

"Not a clue, but I want to find something we can use to convince a judge to allow us to put a tracker on Davis' truck. I still think he's dirty."

"No argument from me. I thought he was a creep from the time we went to his shop. Strange duck," Lisa added.

After their second cup of coffee, Karen brought a plate over and placed it down in front of Lisa. The plate had nine fried eggs on it. This was followed by a second plate, which had six slices of bread and at least a dozen strips of bacon.

As Lisa stared at the mountain of food, Karen announced with a wide smile, "Clay, yours will be right up in a few minutes. Lisa, dig in."

"Very funny. I see your husband isn't the only smart-aleck in the family."

"Smart aleck? Who are you, and what did you do with the real Lisa?" Clay asked.

125

"You two should start your own Vegas act. You're regular comedians," Lisa said as Karen gave Clay a high-five.

Thirty minutes later, as Lisa was clearing the table and Clay was doing dishes, Lisa said, "Now that I won't be able to walk because I ate so much, you wanna get going?"

"Thank you so much for a wonderful breakfast Karen," Lisa said.

"It was our pleasure. You know you are always welcome here. Now go catch bad guys."

As Lisa climbed in the truck with Clay, she turned and said, "I hope you know how cool your wife is, but someday Karen will get her eyesight back and will take one look at you and run."

"Wow! Another comedian, but you're right. She is awesome, and she's a very lucky woman to be married to me."

"Should have brought my hip boots. It's getting a little deep in here," Lisa answered.

About a half-hour after leaving Clay's house, they were at the 2320 road.

"How far back does this road go before it dead-ends?" Lisa asked.

"About three or four miles. It just goes out through this reprod (short for reproduction- young trees) timber until it comes out at a large landing (a flat spot where logs are stacked before being loaded onto trucks)," Clay answered. "I would like to slowly drive the road to the end. Then if we didn't see anything, I will walk the way out, and you can pick me up when I'm done."

126

"Works for me, but maybe at your age, you should sit in the truck while I walk the three or four miles. We don't need you straining your prostate or anything."

"Wow, are you on a roll today. I take it you normally drink decaf coffee, not our high-octane stuff?" Clay countered.

The banter continued non-stop as the wardens crept down the road, staring out their respective open side windows of the truck. Finally, they arrived at the landing.

The only thing Clay noticed at the landing was a campfire ring for a fire someone had weeks ago. Other than the fire-ring, the only thing they saw was the normal bits and pieces of litter found on most public lands.

"Okay, so it took them about six or seven minutes to drive in here from where the camera is. The drive in and out takes up twelve minutes of the twenty-two. That only leaves ten minutes here. They didn't have much time for a hike in the woods," Lisa noted.

"You're right. I was thinking we should be looking for a game trail, but they really didn't have enough time to go for much of a walk. So, what the hell were they doing here?"

"If you will take a real good look all around this landing, I will start walking out. If you find anything, let me know. I will have my portable (radio) on TAC-4," Clay suggested to Lisa.

"See you at the end, unless I fall and break a hip or something."

127

"Keep working on your material. You're not quite ready for Vegas yet."

As Lisa exited the truck and slowly, gently closed her door, Clay grinned. The vast majority of newer officers—which to Clay was anyone with less than fifteen years on the job—Clay had worked with slammed the car doors when they got out, which is a great warning signal to anyone you might be trying to sneak up on. Lisa exited a truck like a real game warden—silently.

As Clay began his walk down the road, Lisa scoured over the landing and then walked out anything that even resembled a trail for at least ten minutes before returning to the landing. But, she found nothing.

Clay completed the 3.3 miles in just over an hour and came up with the same results as Lisa.

"I'm at the intersection," Clay told Lisa over the radio.

"Be there in a few," Lisa responded.

Clay had been sitting on a dirt bank at the intersection for about five minutes when he heard the truck coming out.

While waiting for Lisa, Clay had removed the memory card from the camera on that road, so after climbing back in the truck, he downloaded the photos. He then wiped the memory card clean and returned it to the camera.

He scanned through the six photos, but all were photos of various animals walking by the camera. There were no more vehicles.

128

"I don't get it," said Clay.

"That makes two of us. We need to get a tracker on Davis' truck. He's the only thing close to a suspect that we have," Clay said. "I think it's bullshit that we have to get a search warrant to put a tracker on someone's truck when they won't even know it's there. It doesn't hurt a thing."

"At the academy, they taught us about this brand-new thing called civil liberties. Probably didn't have them around when you went through in the '30s, but you should check them out sometime."

"Thank you very much, Professor Bennington."

"Well, now what, oh wise one?" Lisa asked.

"Hell, I don't know. The only thing I can think of doing that we haven't done so far is to start working nights. Clearly, there is activity at night, but we have no idea what it is."

"I know Emily would like it better if I was on nights too, so let's do it. Let me know when and where, and I will be there," Lisa said.

"I can't do it tomorrow night, but Thursday through Sunday, I'm wide open," Clay responded. "Let's poke around in here Thursday night. Will seven at my place work?"

"You got it. What have you got tomorrow night?" Lisa asked.

"It's the "meet your local game warden" night at hunter education class," Clay answered.

129

"I thought Sean was going to take all of the admin crap so that we could focus on this case," Lisa said.

"It won't work for this because it's meet a game warden night, not meet an administrator in the making night. Besides, I like doing it. Always great to see a bunch of kids excited about something other than video games."

"Have you ever driven with NGV's on?" Clay asked.

"Haven't had the experience yet."

"How about changing that on Thursday. You want to drive?"

"Why not. I am pretty sure my first time driving around at night with no lights on will be far safer than riding with you on a warm sunny day anytime," Lisa said.

"You know you just jinxed yourself with that trash talk. I should probably wear a helmet on Thursday."

They were about three miles from Oroville on the way back to Clay's house when Lisa's phone rang.

"A voice from the past. It's my old sarge," Lisa said when she saw the name on her phone.

"It's been too long, kid," Sgt. Tim Greene said.

"Agreed. How have you been?" Lisa asked.

"I'm perfect as always, and I assume the same with you?"

"Absolutely. So, to what do I owe the honor?" Lisa asked.

130

"Yesterday, I, along with the other region four sergeants, had the pleasure of spending all day being enlightened by our gifted and truly inspirational captain."

"Oh, how I do miss those short six-hour region four meetings," Lisa said with a smirk.

"Anyway, about halfway through the meeting, the chief showed up to give us the state of the department update. One of the things he addressed was the poaching spree you guys are dealing with. He said it now looks like a commercial bear gall operation."

"Yep, it's sure starting to look that way," Lisa confirmed.

"We had the same thing going on over here: deer being used for bear bait and the whole thing. None of us had ever seen deer used for bear bait like that, but it sure as hell seemed to work because the guy was whacking the hell out of our bear," Sgt. Greene said.

"It sure sounds like the same thing you have going on there, with one big difference," Greene added.

"And what's that?"

"We caught our guy."

"No shit! Is he in custody?" Lisa asked.

"Wake up, girl. Remember, this is King County, where nobody actually ever goes to jail. He was admin booked and then released the same day. He ended up getting zero jail time and $4,300 in fines and penalties, which he will never pay. But, I thought you might be interested in the case."

131

"Absolutely. Can you shoot me a copy of your case report?" Lisa asked.

"To keep you out of trouble, I will email it to your sergeant and ask him to share it with you. Your boy seems to be one of those guys who gets all wound up about the important shit like chain-of-command and policy."

"You've got that right. Thanks."

"And tell that dinosaur you work with, I said hi."

"He heard that, and I won't pass on his response because it was totally inappropriate," Lisa said.

"That's funny, I never heard him say a word, and Clay has never been one who was accused of being soft-spoken," Greene said back.

"Well, if he had said something, it would have been totally inappropriate," Lisa responded.

"I don't doubt it for a second. Hey, you guys take care of yourselves, and if you ever get tired of hillbillies and cowboys, there is always a spot back here for you."

"Thanks, and say hi to everyone for me," Lisa said.

"Will do kid. Be careful."

CHAPTER 21

It was exactly two-hundred and thirty-four miles from his house to the Sandpoint Idaho Wal-Mart. He loved this drive and the easy money it brought in. About once a month, he made the trip and always by himself. The boss had always told him to obey all of the traffic laws, with no exception other than he was allowed to go up to five mph over the speed limit. This didn't bother him at all on this drive. He loved the scenery.

Every time he came to Sandpoint, he said he was going to come back just to spend a couple of days checking the area out. He liked Idaho a whole lot better than Washington and someday wanted to move there.

Craig always allowed extra time, just in case he had a problem along the way, so on this day, he was an hour and twenty minutes early for the meet. Craig decided to hit the Sandpoint Restaurant and Brew Pub for a rack of baby-back ribs, something he liked to do almost every trip. He wanted a beer, but his boss had warned him about the six B's at least a dozen times. Craig wasn't really worried about his boss because the guy seemed pretty mellow, but it was the big boss he feared.

Craig had never met the "Rainman," as everyone called him, but he had heard stories, and they weren't good. He still remembered his boss once telling him that if he ever broke the six B's rules and got caught, he would be far better off just staying in jail. Apparently, the Rainman wasn't a very forgiving guy.

At exactly 12:51, Craig saw the metallic grey Toyota, with a large wooden dog box in the back, pull into the Wal-Mart parking lot. As usual, the small truck circled the entire parking lot before pulling alongside Craig's truck.

"Well, let's see what you've got," Craig said to the houndsman.

The man handed a plastic bag out the window to Craig, who carefully opened the bag to inspect the frozen contents.

"Man, a couple of these are pretty damned small, and you have a couple I see still have some liver tissue attached. Not sure the boss will even want those," Craig said.

"I count fourteen good ones, two that are marginal, and three that are total crap. I'll give you a grand for all of them," Craig told the hunter.

"Fifteen-hundred," The hound-hunter replied.

Craig counted out twelve one-hundred-dollar bills, put them in a mailing envelope, and handed it to the houndsman.

"There's twelve-hundred dollars cash in there, and that's the best I can do."

"Deal," the hunter said as he took the envelope. "Until next time."

As Craig turned to reverse the route he had just taken, he chuckled to himself. He had just bought nineteen perfectly good bear gallbladder for about sixty-three bucks each. Craig did the math. Nineteen gallbladders, at an average of about 180 grams each, are

134

thirty-four hundred and twenty dollars. Multiply that by the buck and a quarter he got per gram, and he was up to forty-two hundred and seventy-five bucks. By the time he got back to Omak, even if he had subtracted the gas money and lunch, he would be up at least twenty-nine hundred dollars credit for one day's work. God bless Idaho!

CHAPTER 22

Knowing that tonight was their first night shift, Clay wanted to sleep in, but instead, he awoke at his normal 5:30. Karen was still in bed when Clay started a pot of coffee and fired up his state computer. Once again Sgt. Sean had saved the day. He had miraculously obtained case reports from several officers in region four who had made a great bear poaching case and passed the reports on to Clay and Lisa.

"Couldn't have done it without you, Sergeant Sean," Clay muttered to himself as he opened the case reports.

As Clay worked further and further through the case reports, he realized what a great job the west-side wardens had done. It truly was an amazing investigation.

The case began on the first Tuesday of September last year when one of the officers received a citizen's complaint of an illegal bear bait, which he had found while was cruising timber (a method of systematically walking through the timber while determining forest health, size, and distribution). The RP (reporting party) had stumbled into the bear bait by accident when he had walked about three-quarters of a mile into the forest from the road. He first spotted the dead deer, which was tied by cable to a tree and near a pile of fish heads. He looked around the area and spotted a tree stand within 40 yards, providing a clear line of sight to the bait.

The timber cruiser backed out of the area and immediately called the poaching hotline to report his find.

136

Officer Zach Edwards, a new officer with only two years on the job, initially took the call and met the RP, who provided him with photos he had taken of the site, as well as the GPS coordinates. Once the RP had taken the officer to the bait, he said goodbye and returned to his forestry duties.

Zach first just took in the whole scene, getting an idea of how to go about processing it. He then began photographing the scene, which was when he first noticed the trail camera pointed directly at the bait pile. Zach knew the camera's presence meant a totally different approach was necessary. Before finding the camera, he would have left everything in place, hoping to catch the poacher in the act. The camera would obviously now have photos of both the forester and Zach since they had both stood right in front of the bait. He simply gloved up, unbuckled the camera from the tree, and set it by his evidence kit.

Next, Zach started inspecting the ground around the bait, where he found large quantities of bear hair and blood. Apparently, the hunter had been successful, but he had used illegal bait to lure the animal in. Zach took tissue samples, blood samples, hair samples and removed a .22 caliber bullet from the skull of the deer. As Zach dug the bullet from the deer, he noticed the drag marks heading downhill from the bait. Once he had the .22 round out of the deer, Zach began following the drag marks, which ended at a dead bear about 40 yards from the bait. Another carcass and another bullet were added to the evidence recovered at the scene.

Once Zach was done processing the scene, he returned to the truck, where he downloaded the trail camera's photos onto his

137

department laptop. When he opened the first photo, out of the forty-seven on the memory card, he yelled, "Got ya," and then picked up the phone to call his sarge.

"I'm up at that bait we got the call on."

"Okay, what's up?" Sgt. Greene asked.

"Well, the guy definitely killed at least one bear and one deer that I know of for sure. He was using the deer and some salmon carcasses as bait. He also has a really nice tree stand and a high-quality trail camera. I just downloaded the trail cam pics, and you will never guess what's on there," Zach told his sergeant.

"Photos of the poacher setting up the trail cam?" Greene asked.

"Way to rain on my parade. I'm guessing this isn't a first, then?"

"Nope. Sorry, but that's not uncommon. Do you know who the guy is?"

"Nah, nobody I recognize, but I thought I would send the photo around and see if I can come up with a name," Zach replied.

"When you are done up there, why don't you meet me at the detachment office," Greene said.

"Will do."

"Hey, one more thing. Since you have all of the photos downloaded, why don't you place that same trail camera along the road, so you can pick up the license plates of anyone who comes back there? Get some plate numbers, and we can run the registered owners

138

to see if any of them match the guy on the trail cam. While I'm waiting for you, I will see if I can find a couple of the department trail cameras. Then you can go back and swap out the cameras," Greene instructed Officer Edwards. "The bad guy doesn't know we found his bait, so he will be back."

"Holy crap, did you just come up with that yourself?"

"Sometimes it's a gift to be this brilliant, and other times it's a curse," Sgt. Greene said as he ended the call.

As Zach was strapping the suspect's own trail camera to a tree, he realized he had not finished looking at the other forty-six photos.

Once back in his truck, Zach opened the photo file again and browsed through the entire set. Zach found three more photos of the hunter adding fish to the bait pile and seven photos of a bear coming into the bait. The remainder of the photos were of other wildlife or tree limbs moving because of wind. Because the camera was aimed directly at the bait site, it would not have picked up the poacher if he had come directly to the tree stand and back.

Zach had come back to the detachment office only to find two trail cameras in the center of the conference table.

"Merry Christmas, courtesy of SIU," Sgt. Greene told Zach.

"So, what do you suggest we do next?" Zach asked.

"You probably should swap out the cameras as soon as you can because there is a chance you can get prints off of it, especially on the batteries. I will forward the best photo of the suspect to all of our guys

139

and anyone else we can trust to keep their mouths shut. The only way we blow this now is if the guy knows we are coming," Greene added.

"Next, I would suggest checking the times and days of the week the suspect is coming into the site. That might tell you if he has a pattern. Lastly, and depending on how bad you want this guy, you could sit on the bait until he shows back up because once he gets into the site, he is going to know someone was there, and then he's going to go home and get rid of everything," Greene added.

"I want this guy bad," Zach answered.

"Then get to work, and when you have a schedule worked out, we will look for volunteers, but you and I get the best shifts. I want to be there when you put cuffs on this boy."

Altogether, the memory card had four photos of the poacher. All four were taken at first daylight and on weekdays.

"I want to be in place tomorrow by five a.m.," Zach said.

"Okay then, send me your best photos of the suspect, go up and swap the trail camera, log the poacher's camera into evidence with the rest of the evidence, and I will meet you here at 4:00 tomorrow morning" said Greene.

"Cool, see you in the morning!"

Zach sent the Sarge the best photo, which Greene sent to the entire region, along with a request for volunteers to work on the stakeout of the bait. Without exception, every member of Zach's detachment volunteered to be used at any time they were needed, so

140

Zach made up a schedule, which he emailed to all involved. Zach knew they wouldn't need the schedule because he felt certain that he and the Sarge would catch the guy in the morning tomorrow.

Wednesday came and went with no success, as did Thursday, and then on Friday morning, it was back to Zach and Sgt. Greene.

On Friday morning, Zach was sitting in camouflage, staring at the bear bait, when at about 6:15, Sgt. Greene, who was positioned out a side road about a half-mile from the trail to the bait site, called and said they had an incoming vehicle. Unfortunately, Sgt. Greene couldn't see the driver nor the license plate, but he knew there was only one way out, and it was to come right back out past him, which wasn't going to happen because he had just pulled his truck out of hiding and parked it directly across the narrow logging road, blocking it entirely. He then grabbed his AR-15 and began walking toward the trail to the bait site, stopping just around the corner from the trail.

Greene had told Zach to click his microphone three times when the poacher was visible to him.

Zach got more and more nervous as the time passed. He started asking himself what had gone wrong as he was certain the guy wasn't coming to the bait. He suddenly really had to pee, but he didn't want the bad guy walking in when he was otherwise occupied.

Maybe it wasn't the poacher in the truck the Sarge had seen, or maybe it was the bad guy, but he saw something just wasn't right and kept going. Something must have been wrong.

141

Zach's watch said 6:43 when he first saw the poacher coming toward the bait site. Zach's hands shook as he clicked his mic three times. The poacher was in full camo from head to toe and even had painted his face. He carried a scoped rifle at the ready and a hunting pack on his back. As the hunter got closer, Zach could see how skinny he was. The guy was emaciated and haggard like a drug addict. The poacher moved very slowly and deliberately, picking his footing carefully to avoid stepping on anything which might produce a loud snap. He was actually pretty quiet as he made his way closer. When he arrived at the tree with the stand in it, he took his pack off and dropped it to the ground.

The poacher then stood perfectly still—as if he had heard something. Zach might have missed any sounds other than that of his own heartbeat because that literally was all he could hear. Zach was both scared and excited but was absolutely loving the rush of adrenaline. After what seemed like an eternity, the poacher walked slowly toward the bait site. When he got to the site, he began shaking his head side to side and swaying back and forth. It was the missing deer head. Zach had removed the head of the deer to extract the bullet, and the poacher was now looking at the deer's neck. The poacher then stood, brought his rifle up, and started swiveling around in all directions. Even though Zach was also wearing full camouflage and was well concealed, he just knew the poacher would see him. Should he bring his rifle up now too? *Shit, shit, shit,* Zach repeated in his mind.

"Game Warden, drop the gun now!" The unexpected shout just about made Zach pee his pants.

142

He knew it was Sgt. Greene, but he had no idea where Greene was. When he looked back at the poacher, he saw the man was looking at his own chest. At first, Zach wasn't sure what he was seeing as a pinpoint of very intense green light danced around in a two-inch circle in the middle of the poacher's chest. Then a wide smile came across his face as he remembered Sgt. Green had a laser sight mounted on his AR-15.

"Last time I ask. Drop the gun now, or I'll drop you!"

The poacher slowly let the rifle slide out of his hands gently onto the ground.

"Hands on top of your head—palms up! Take ten big steps forward and kneel down! Now cross your feet and sit back on them."

This is so awesome! Zach screamed in his mind. Then it got even better.

"Okay, Officer Edwards, go forward and cuff your prisoner."

Zach rose to his feet, went forward, and cuffed the man exactly as he had been trained to do.

The report Clay had finished reading detailed how the region four officers had apprehended the poacher, as well as his interrogation, the search of his home and vehicle, the poacher's criminal history, and a detailed inventory of all seized items of evidence.

Officers Zach Edwards and Keith Welborne conducted the interrogation of Lee K. Benson at the jail.

143

During the interrogation, the suspect, Mr. Benson, admitted to having already killed three different bears in the last month. When asked where the gallbladders were going, Benson refused to answer. He confessed to illegally killing three black bears and five different deer. He admitted to the wastage of the deer and bear meat. He admitted to selling bear gallbladder, but when it came to who was buying the gallbladder, he wouldn't answer the question.

Mr. Benson had one felony conviction for trafficking in heroin, as well as six misdemeanor convictions, two of which were game violations.

The poacher's written statement was enough to put him in jail for a long time, but being in King County, nobody held any hope of that happening. In fact, a quick check of Benson's current status showed he had been released from custody two days after the wardens had arrested him. He had been provided with a public defender, who was able to get the prosecutor to drop eight of the ten criminal charges, including unlawful possession of a firearm by a convicted felon and possession of heroin, the wardens had filed with the prosecutor.

The poacher was allowed to plead to one count of unlawful hunting of big game and unlawful possession of a firearm, and he was given a 365-day sentence with all but two days suspended. The court then gave Benson credit for time served, which meant he would not spend another day in jail on these charges and $10,000 in fines and penalties. The amount of heroin found by the officers in Benson's home was not enough to meet King County's minimum threshold for heroin possession. Clay had never before heard of a county ignoring possession of heroin, no matter what the amount, but King County was another beast entirely.

The state had seized Benson's firearms, and vehicle, which were forfeited to the department of fish and wildlife, and Benson's hunting privileges were once again suspended.

When the officers initially arrested Benson, they found he carried two different phones. Officer Edwards had obtained warrants to search both phones as well as records with the phone service provider. Once served with the warrants, Benson agreed to open the phones for the officers, hoping to gain brownie points with the prosecutor by way of his cooperation.

One phone, an I-phone, had dozens of incriminating photos of Benson posing with poached animals and a multitude of text messages and phone calls as well as fifty-seven people in his contacts list. The second phone, an LG Rebel FlashFone, had only one contact with one number and no photos or text messages. The phone number found in the FlashFone contacts list also came back as a FlashFone. Since the FlashFone is a disposable burner, the company could not tell the officers who currently possessed the phone.

In a desperate effort to learn the identity of who had the other FlashFone, Zach sent it a text: "What have you been up to lately?" But, the text went unanswered.

Clay opened his email program and typed out a quick email to Officer Edwards. He cc'd Lisa.

Zach, I just completed reading your case report on Benson, and I wanted to tell you what an outstanding job you did. Congratulations! Do you think it would be possible to set up another interview with Mr. Benson? Lisa Bennington and I have been working on a large-scale bear poaching case over here, and I think Benson might be able to help us out if we can entice him into cooperation. Secondly, did you ever ask FlashFone where that particular cell phone was sold?

I look forward to your response, and once again, great work! Clay.

Clay shut down his computer and sat back, mulling over the westside case.

It has to be connected to what's happening here, but does that mean it's being run out of the westside or here somewhere? Clay thought. *We just need to find the common thread between these cases.*

In the late afternoon, Clay checked his email again and found Officer Edwards had replied.

Officer Newberry: I will work on contacting Mr. Benson today, and if I can locate him, I will get you a contact number, but I wouldn't hold your breath. The guy was terrified of whoever he was selling gall to, and he's a heroin addict, but I will try. No, I never even thought of asking where the FlashFone was sold, which was a screw-up on my part. Since it was almost a year ago, I seriously doubt any judge would grant me a warrant now, so all I can say is sorry. I will get back to you as soon as I know something about Benson. Zach.

Clay immediately emailed Zach again.

146

Zach: Thanks, but mellow out on the FlashFone thing. If I had been in your shoes, I wouldn't have asked for those records either. You did a great job, and I wouldn't criticize you for one single thing on the way you handled the case. Thanks again. Clay.

These disposable phones were tailor-made made for criminals, Clay thought. *If the cellular phone companies really cared about criminals using their phones to evade capture, they would simply require purchasers to provide photo IDs upon purchase and would require vendors to keep records of who bought which phones.*

The cell phone companies that produce these phones should be charged with rendering criminal aid.

147

CHAPTER 23

The Forensic Laboratory Services Bureau (FLSB) of the
Washington State Patrol (WSP) handles the vast majority of forensics
evidence for law enforcement agencies from across the state.
Forensics DNA of wildlife was done in-house by WDFW's own DNA
lab, but virtually everything else went to the WSP "crime lab" (as it is
called by most officers). The FLSB had labs in Seattle, Spokane,
Tacoma, Marysville, Vancouver, Kennewick, and Olympia. The
various labs all seemed to specialize in different facets of forensics
analysis. All forensic toxicology services were conducted in the
toxicology lab in Seattle, while the Spokane lab handled firearms/tool
marks examination, seized drug analysis, and latent prints analysis.

Washington State Patrol Forensic Scientist, Trisha Sanchez, had
completed the documentation on the fingerprint analysis of a shell
casing, which had been submitted by Moses Lake Police, and she was
ready to examine the next piece of evidence on her list.

This evidence consisted of a six by eight-foot tarp, along with four
strips of layered duct tape. Trisha opted to explore the tape first. For
the first step in the process, Trisha needed one of the other scientists to
help. Trisha's assistant dripped a 2% solution of chloroform tape
release agent where the two layers of tape came together while Trisha
gently pulled the tape strips apart. When all four strips of layered tape
had been separated, Trisha had ten separate tape strips. She then laid
the strips side by side, adhesive side up, photographed them, and then
left them to dry for twenty-four hours.

After that task was completed, Trisha moved onto the tarp, which, as she expected, had only smeared unusable prints. The tarp did, however, have some bloodstains, which she determined were blood from an American Black Bear.

The next day, Trisha returned to the tape strips where she applied adhesive-side developer, which she then rinsed off after just seconds. When completed, Trisha could see over a dozen high-quality fingerprints, which she then photographed and covered with clear tape. The last step in the analysis was to enter the fingerprints into AFIS (Automated Fingerprint Identification System).

When the fingerprints had been analyzed by AFIS, all of the prints came back to one person: Hamill, Blake Eugene—D.O.B. (date of birth) 06-24-93. Blake had a fairly insignificant criminal history with only two arrests: one for shoplifting and a second for D.U.I. He had a valid Washington driver's license with an Omak, Washington address.

Trisha completed the analysis report and placed it in the outgoing tray on the counter. The report would be mailed to the submitting officer: Detective Dave Carpenter, with the Okanogan County Sheriff's Office.

CHAPTER 24

At 6:45 p.m., Lisa arrived at Clay's front door. She knocked briefly and then poked her head in, "Hello?"

"Come on in. I'm just getting my uniform on," Clay yelled out.

"Well, by all means, please complete that task before you step out here," Lisa replied.

"Hey punk, you could always wait in the car," Clay shouted.

"Lisa, just ignore the old grouch. It works for me," Karen said.

"I can hear you."

As Clay and Lisa headed out the door, Karen asked, "When do you think you will be back?"

"When we catch the guy," Clay answered.

"Great. I guess we will see you in a couple of months then," added Lisa.

"Wow, Miss Sunshine, your negativity is bringing me down," Clay said with a smile, "And I'm the grouch?"

"Get out of here, you two, and go catch bad guys," Karen said as she kissed Clay goodbye. "Be careful."

"Always," Clay responded.

"Are you up for learning to drive at night without lights?" Clay asked.

"It can't be any worse than your everyday driving," Lisa answered.

"Okay, let's head up the 23 Mainline and poke around there for a while."

"You've got it, boss."

"You get a chance to read about that case they made in your old detachment?" Clay asked.

"I did, and they did a great job. That must have been pretty exciting for Zach. He was always high-strung. You made a good point about finding where the cell phone was sold, but it's just our luck that nobody went after that information and that the suspect croaked. Dead-ends all the way around, no pun intended."

"What do you mean about the suspect being dead?" Clay asked.

"Oh, you didn't see Zach's follow-up email. Apparently, Mr. Benson, the poacher, died of an accidental drug overdose three weeks ago. A combination of alcohol, heroin, and fentanyl."

"Guess I'm not too sorry to hear that. I just wish he had waited until after we got a chance to talk to him," Clay responded.

Clay and Lisa arrived at the 23 Mainline just as it was getting dark. Lisa pulled to the side of the road, reached to the backseat, pulled out the NVGs, and asked, "Okay, show me how these things work."

The ATN PS15-WPT Night Vision Goggles were top of the line. The goggles employed two separate WPT (White Phosphor

151

Technology) intensifier tubes, which provide the user with a much-improved field of vision and increased depth perception. The goggles also have an automatic bright light cut-off, which protects the goggles from damage caused by exposure to bright light. Like most goggles, the ATN PS15-WPT goggles came with IR (Infrared) illuminators, which are invisible to the naked eye, but, when used with NVGs, lights up targets even in total darkness.

All WDFW patrol vehicles are equipped with a "cut-out switch." When activated, this will disconnect the truck's brake lights to allow officers to drive completely blacked out. Many officers will also tape over the dash lights for total darkness.

"Okay, this dial is the only control. You have a choice of Off, On, or IR. In IR mode, you will see a bright light, like a floodlight, everywhere you look, but that light is invisible without the goggles. IR is only needed when there is no ambient light from stars or the moon. Before we start, switch off the brake lights with your cut-out switch. Next, take this electrical tape and tape over every little glowing light you can see in here, especially on the dash," Clay instructed.

"Now comes the fun part. Slip these onto your head, and then use this dial in the back of the harness to adjust the tightness. You will want it as tight as you can stand it."

"Okay, got it," Lisa responded.

"So, what do you think?" Clay asked as Lisa checked out her surroundings with the goggles.

"Holy shit. This is amazing."

152

"All right, now the two negatives about these. You will find your depth perception is skewed with these, but you will get used to it. Just be aware of it. Next, bright lights—like when a vehicle suddenly lights you up with headlights—will temporarily blind you because the goggles will automatically shut down to keep them from being damaged. So, if you see a vehicle coming toward us, switch the goggles off and stop the truck. Are you ready?"

"Yep," Lisa said began rolling down the roadway. "This is kind of spooky."

"You want to try spooky, sit on the passenger side while the driver has NVGs, and you don't. You have no idea what's coming next in the road, so you just sit there hurling through the darkness in sheer terror. At least when you're driving."

As Lisa got the hang of driving with the goggles, she picked up more and more speed until finally, she was going about the same speed as she would have with headlights on.

"Now, find a place to back our truck in, where we won't be spotted, and let's follow the next vehicle that comes by," Clay said.

After nearly three hours of waiting Lisa could see the glow of a vehicle coming their way. Soon the Nissan pickup passed by them, and it was Lisa's turn to go. She started the truck, turned the goggles on, and began following.

"The road dust makes it tough to see," Lisa commented.

"It would even if you were driving with headlights. You will get used to it."

153

Lisa learned that if she backed off just a bit more, she could see the road better and could still see where the truck they were following went. It got easier and easier the further they went.

"How far do you want to follow this guy?" Lisa asked.

"I've got nothing else to do. Let's just follow him until we know what he's doing."

Lisa had followed the truck for fifteen minutes when she saw that it had taken a right onto an unmarked side road. As Lisa got to the intersection of the side road and the 23 Mainline, she stopped.

"What's going on? Why did we stop?" Clay asked.

"It's lit up like a football stadium ahead. I have no idea what all of that is."

"Take off your goggles and take a look," Clay suggested.

"Wow, you can barely see any light at all without the goggles. Take a look at what I mean," Lisa said as she passed the goggles to Clay.

"I see what you are talking about, and I have no idea what that is, so let's go see," Clay said as he passed the goggles back to Lisa.

Once Lisa had the goggles on again, they continued down the narrow road. The further they went, the brighter the glow was ahead.

Finally, they rounded a left-hand corner and found themselves looking at a large campfire surrounded by at least a dozen high school-aged kids.

154

Lisa took her goggles off and realized she could now see the group clearly without the aid of the NVGs. Lisa then joined Clay in looking at the group with binoculars. Lisa noticed that all but a few kids had cans of beer in their hands. She and Clay discussed how to handle the situation, all while the kids were oblivious to their presence.

"Light 'em up," Clay said.

Lisa simultaneously turned on her headlights and her emergency lights as she hurriedly drove to the edge of the group. The teens stood frozen like deer in the headlights.

As they walked into the middle of the group, Clay realized he knew the majority of them because they were all from Oroville.

Once everyone had quieted down, Clay addressed the group. "Okay, we are going to form three lines, starting right here. The first line is for those of you who admit you have been drinking and are underage. The next line is for those of you who honestly haven't been drinking and for anyone over the age of twenty-one. That should be a pretty short line. The last line is for those who have been drinking but are going to try to lie to us and say they weren't. Now let's all line up."

Lisa was amazed that eleven kids lined up in the "I admit I was drinking" line, two kids lined up at the "I didn't drink at all" line, and nobody lined up at the "I've been drinking and am going to lie about it" line.

"Very good. Now I want everyone to get their IDs out and hand them to Officer Bennington."

155

Clay then pointed at the two girls who had stood in the "I haven't been drinking line" and asked them to follow him to the truck. At the truck, Clay removed Lisa's PBT (Portable Breath Test) and asked each girl to submit a voluntary breath sample. Both girls agreed to do so, and both blew perfect .000 readings.

"We are the designated drivers," one of the girls declared.

"Good decision," Lisa answered.

"Are we going to jail?" one of the boys asked.

"Raise your hand if you have ever been charged with a drug or alcohol violation, and don't forget we will find out as soon as we run you," Lisa warned.

Nobody raised their hands.

"Here's the deal, guys. I was ready to call the county and get them to bring up the transport van to take all of you to jail, but Officer Bennington talked me out of it. She said a MIP (Minor in possession of alcohol) arrest might keep you out of certain careers and/or colleges, so we have an offer for you," Clay said.

"As long as you do not have any prior drug or alcohol arrests, we will let you off with a warning tonight, but there are two conditions of release: First, we are going to speak to each and every one of your parents, and that's not up for debate. Secondly, you owe us one now. As you guys all know, someone is going around shooting and leaving wildlife all over the hills. You now owe us information. If you hear of anything that might help us catch whoever is doing this, you will have to tell us about it. Does anyone want to pass on the offer?" Clay asked.

156

"While you guys are waiting your turn, I want all of the beer and anything else you have poured out right now. Also, make sure this place is cleaner than when you got here. I hate litterbugs," Clay instructed the group.

Nobody balked at the offer, so one by one, Lisa ran every kid while Clay took down their parents' names and contact numbers. Once they were done, Lisa made the final announcement.

"You have four vehicles here. Your two designated drivers can drive whatever vehicles you agree to let them drive and can drive you right to your homes. For those of you who have a car here and have been drinking, you can leave the car here until tomorrow, or you can get two sober drivers to come up here to drive your car back for you. Make no mistake; if we see any of you who have been drinking out driving tonight, we will seize your car and lock you up. Clear?" Lisa said.

"Now, does anyone need us to drive you home?" Clay asked.

The group gave a unanimous "no" to the offer of a ride with the wardens.

"Okay, guys, use your brains from now on, and don't put yourselves in a position where someone is going to drive home drunk. It's just not worth it," Lisa added as they walked back to their patrol vehicle.

"Thanks," said one of the kids. "Yeah, thanks a lot for not busting us. We owe you," said another.

With that, Clay and Lisa were done with the contact.

157

"Well, what do you think of how that went?" Clay asked.

"I'm not sure a verbal warning will do the job at deterring similar behavior in the future, but they all did seem like good kids."

"I don't even have to ask if you did the same thing in high school because I know you did. Hell, everyone did. So, just think what would have happened to your career in law enforcement if you had a MIP and/or a DUI on your record," Clay said. "I got caught in high school by a city cop while I was drinking and smoking pot. The fact that he let me off with a warning after telling my parents was the reason I was able to get this career. It was also the same reason I was grounded by my parents for three months of high school."

"I'm serious about calling their parents, which I will do tomorrow. Some won't care at all. One or two will ask me why I'm not chasing real criminals, and the rest will thank us and assure us we will never have that problem with their child again. We may even get a written apology from a kid or two. This wasn't the first party I've ruined."

"What do you want to do for the rest of the night?" Lisa asked.

"Let's move south and find a high spot just to sit on and watch for lights and listen for shots," Clay suggested.

"I know just the spot. Hang on. I'm going to see if I can make you scream like a little girl," Lisa said as she pulled back onto the 23 Mainline.

The remainder of the night was uneventful, so at four a.m., they called it a night and headed back into town. Lisa was driving like it

158

was daytime and was confident in her abilities to run with just the NVGs.

"How about trying down in my area tomorrow night?" Lisa asked.

"Sounds good to me. When do you want me down there?"

"Let's go with 7:00 at my house."

"See ya tomorrow night. Good job tonight," Clay said as he stepped out of Lisa's truck and onto his lawn.

CHAPTER 25

On a quiet Wednesday morning, Rainman's LG Rebel FlashFone cell phone emitted a tone indicating the receipt of a text message. Rainman didn't like text messages and had told his people to only use them for messages which you won't mind having the police read someday because that was always a real possibility in his business.

The text was from his right-hand man, "If you are going to be at work, I would like to swing by and talk to you for a few minutes if that works for you."

"Anytime today. I will be at work all day. Swing on by," Rainman answered while wondering what that was all about. In the three years Mike had worked for him, he had never asked Rainman to have a chat like this.

This can't be good, Rainman thought as he went back to work.

Two hours after the mystery text, Rainman saw Mike coming his way. "So, my friend, what's so important you came all this way today?" Rainman asked.

"Kinda hard for me to ask, but here it is," Mike said. "You already know I'm getting married in less than a month."

Rainman nodded his head in response.

"Well, she has two kids and all, and we were talking. Her dad owns that huge apple orchard, he's in poor health and has offered me a job running the orchard. It doesn't pay as well as this, but there is zero risk of ending up in prison or dead, which are two real possibilities in

160

our business. So, I'm hoping you would be okay with me getting out of this business—for good."

After a few seconds of pause, Rainman responded, "As long as you forget everything about me and our operation, I have no problem at all with your retirement. You have always served me well, and I have nothing but trust for you. Of course, you have my blessing, but I would ask that you give me a few weeks to find a replacement."

"That's more than fair, sir," Mike said as he shook Rainman's hand. "To be honest, I didn't know how this conversation would go over. I kind of wondered if I might end up with a large hole in my head."

"I consider you family and would never allow harm to come to you or your family. As a matter of fact, I want you and your new bride to pick a honeymoon destination anywhere and let me know where it is. Your honeymoon is on me, my friend."

"That's very generous, sir. Thank you. I will talk it over with my fiancé and let you know."

"Do you have a replacement in mind?" Mike asked.

"I do, and I just need to put him through a few more tests first to make sure," Rainman answered.

"Who?"

"There's one drawback to retiring from the business. You no longer have access to that kind of information," Rainman said with a grin.

161

CHAPTER 26

Clay pulled into Lisa's driveway a few minutes before 7:00 p.m. and saw Emily out playing with their dog, Mayhem.

"How's it going, Emily?" Clay asked as he petted Mayhem.

"It's been busy, but I understand you know the feeling."

"I would say busy is good, but I guess in our line of work, that's not always a good thing," Clay answered.

"True enough," Emily replied. "Sounds like you two have determined the motivation for all of this poaching is commercial?"

"Yep, it sure looks that way."

"I had never heard of the bear gallbladder thing until Lisa told me, and now that's all I hear about. I hope you two catch these guys soon so that we can have conversations about normal things from then on," Emily said.

"Oh yeah, normal things like meth labs, child molesters, and murder," Clay added.

"Touché."

Lisa came out of the house carrying a gear bag, which she put in the back seat of her patrol vehicle.

"You ready?" She asked Clay.

"Let's hit it," he answered.

162

"You kids, be careful," Emily said as they both got into Lisa's truck.

"Well, where to, young lady?" Clay asked.

"I was thinking of concentrating on that area around Dead Horse Ridge."

"Works for me."

Lisa knew the area much better than Clay's area and already knew where she wanted to wait, watch, and listen. She had picked a spot that gave them a panoramic view of the valley below, including the road where she and Clay had processed the recent poaching scene.

More for practice than any other reason, Lisa donned the NVGs and drove blacked out once they were on gravel roads. After twenty minutes of driving, Clay felt the vehicle slow and turn a hard right. It then came to a stop in a place where he could see the lights in downtown Omak.

"We should be able to see any vehicle that comes in the way we did, but off to the south, there are at least three other roads that will bring you up here. We won't be able to see most of that, but we've sure got this side covered," Lisa said.

As the night wore on, Lisa and Clay noted the times when they had seen the vehicles moving around below them. From this distance, they couldn't tell what kind of vehicles they were, but they knew there were at least three of them down there somewhere. They decided they were far better off waiting to see if anyone was using a spotlight and

163

listening for shots before they just took off driving around randomly trying to locate the vehicles.

Finally, at 3:17 a.m., both Clay and Lisa heard the shot of a high-powered rifle. Lisa pointed slightly to the north of their position as the location she believed the shot had come from. Clay believed it came from an area a bit further south. After waiting ten minutes for another shot to be fired, which did not occur, they decided to work their way down to try to locate the shooter.

Lisa, driving with the NVGs, worked her way down the hill while scanning the area for any light. Once down in the valley, she decided to take the 2816 road to the south. As she reached each side road, she would ask Clay to get out and check the road for any sign of recent traffic, but the further they drove, the lower their odds were of finding the shooter.

"I don't think there is any way the shot was from this far south. Let's head back to the north and see what's up in that direction," Clay said.

It was just after four when Lisa crossed the Dead Horse Ridge Road and headed north. As the two officers headed north, they went through the same process of checking side roads, but again they found nothing.

"There are just way too many roads here. We aren't going to find them this way," Clay remarked.

"You have a better suggestion?" Lisa asked.

164

"Yeah, but it won't help us tonight. The only hope we have is cameras and more cameras."

"You want to move them down this way?" Lisa asked.

"I think that would be wise. This area has some strange activity going on, so I think we should move every camera we have down here, except for the one on the 2320 road where we saw Matt Davis meeting up with Bradford."

"Works for me. When do you want to get them?" Lisa asked.

"It's getting light now, so let's keep poking around in here, just in case. Then whenever you wake up today, give me a call, and we can go grab them and move them. We will go plainclothes and in the unmarked truck."

At 7:00 a.m., they decided to bag it and head home. As Lisa pulled into her driveway, she asked Clay, "You want to leave the unmarked here for a while? If you aren't available, I could always take Emily up to check the cameras?"

"Sure. I don't think Moe would mind us giving him his shop back. When you come up to move the cameras, just pick me up on your way to Moe's. We can then move it down to your place, and you can run me back up. Sounds like a plan."

"Okay, I'll call you this afternoon. See ya," Lisa said as she walked toward the back door of her home.

CHAPTER 27

In Columbia County, Washington, Deputy Brice McMillan and his family lived in an older but newly remodeled home that depended on the woodstove as its primary heat source. Winters could be brutal and long, and Brice liked to have at least eight cords of firewood cut and stacked in his woodshed. On this day, Brice inspected his nearly empty woodshed and decided it was well past time to spend his off-duty time cutting and splitting firewood. Brice was the second most senior deputy, with twelve years on, and had accrued a good deal of vacation time, some of which he would need to use to resupply his woodshed. Brice had a U.S. Forest Service firewood permit for the Maloney Mountain area and hoped to cut a cord a day on his time off, starting today. Brice got to the area just after 6:30 a.m. but remembered he had to touch up his chain with the file before he started cutting.

Brice pulled up next to a dead and down tree that was perfect, so he turned the truck off and got out to sharpen his saw. As he stepped out of his truck, he immediately heard a pack of hounds, and they sounded like they had something treed. Brice, an avid hunter, knew raccoon season was closed.

Brice decided to check out what was going on, so he started the truck up, turned around, and headed in the direction of the dogs. Before too long, Brice found the road he thought would get him closest to the dogs. When he got as close as he thought the road would take him, Brice locked the chainsaw in the truck and started walking through the dense timber toward the dogs.

It was only 6:43 a.m., but Gregg was still worried there might be someone around there somewhere. The dogs had the big, boar black bear treed, so he had to shut them up before someone noticed. The dogs were loud enough to be heard for miles. The only thing he had left to do was to put a bullet in the bear's head, load the dogs, grab the gallbladder, and get out of there. It should only take him a half-hour or so.

Gregg chambered a round in his lever-action 30-30, aimed just behind the right eye of the bear, and squeezed the trigger. The bear instantly dropped dead, just as he had planned.

Brice knew he was within a hundred yards of the dogs, so he unholstered his Glock and continued on.

The sound of the shot scared the crap out of Brice, but it confirmed that someone was up to no good. Brice slowed his pace to avoid detection. He had never snuck up on a poacher before, but it had to be about the same as sneaking up on a dope grow, and he had done that plenty of times.

Gregg leaned his rifle on a tree while he gathered up the dogs and snapped leads to each dog's collar. He about jumped out of his skin when he heard the command.

"Sheriff's Office. Show me your hands and stay where you are."

Gregg went into pure panic mode. He looked for his rifle, but it was too far away to do him any good now. The man who identified himself as a deputy had gotten to within fifteen yards of him, well before Gregg had a clue he was there. Gregg realized he had nowhere to go.

"I need to see some ID deputy," Gregg said.

Brice reached back, pulled out his badge wallet, and produced both his badge and commission card with his left hand while keeping the pistol trained on him with his right.

"Hey, I'm an officer too. Lower your gun," Gregg commanded in a crackling voice.

"I don't think so, pal. Now, turn around and put your hands on top of your head," Brice commanded the poacher.

Gregg complied with the orders.

As Brice approached the suspect from behind, he holstered his pistol, reached up, and grabbed the suspect's hands by interlocking his fingers through his hair, pulled him backward, and searched him. Brice removed a hunting knife from the suspect's belt and a second knife from his right-front pocket. Next, Deputy McMillan removed the suspect's wallet and told him to kneel.

After unloading the suspect's rifle, he took out his driver's license and read it aloud, "Gregg C. Meadows from Walla Walla. Well, Mr. Meadows, you are under arrest for killing this bear during the closed season. Do you understand me?"

"I understand, but I'm a corrections officer. You have my DOC (Department of Corrections) ID in my wallet. How about some professional courtesy here? Cut me a little slack."

"Shut up, will you. It's hard enough to hear anything with the frigging dogs barking without you running your mouth too."

Brice was already on the phone with his dispatch. He asked for both the local game warden and a deputy to respond to assist. Brice then identified the suspect to dispatch and asked them to run a warrant check on him. The warrant check came back clear—no warrants.

"This will mean my job, you know. I have a wife and a six-year-old son at home. Come on, brother, give me a break. We're on the same team," Gregg begged.

"Stand up. Now grab all of your dogs, and let's get them put away in your truck," Brice said in hopes the poacher would lead him to his truck.

Once Gregg had all of the dogs hooked to leads, he began walking them to the truck as the deputy followed him, carrying Gregg's 30-30 rifle.

Once back at Gregg's truck, Gregg loaded the dogs in the box and then sat on the truck's tailgate. Brice recognized the road they were on and conveyed it to dispatch.

I'm not handcuffing you right now, only because I don't have cuffs with me, but I am going to read you your rights. Brice pulled a Miranda warning card out and read the card word for word to the suspect.

"Do you understand your rights as I have read them to you?"

"Yeah, I understand."

169

"Having those rights in mind, are you willing to talk to us?"

"Why not. What do you want to know?" Gregg asked.

"I think I will leave the questions to our game warden. He should be here in fifteen minutes or so."

Fish and Wildlife Officer Kevin Webber was the first to arrive at the scene. As soon as Kevin exited the vehicle, Brice asked for a set of cuffs, which Kevin tossed to him. Brice quickly handcuffed and searched the suspect again, just to make sure he hadn't missed anything.

"Well, what do we have here?" Kevin asked Brice.

"Shove him in your cage, and I will show you," Brice answered.

"The guy was alone?" Kevin asked.

"Yep, no sign of anyone else, and the passenger seat in his truck is covered with hunting equipment. It sure doesn't look like anyone rode up here with him," Brice responded.

The cage in Kevin's patrol truck was made of steel and plexiglass and took up half of the truck's backseat. Most importantly, the cage held prisoners securely and was difficult to escape from, especially if the prisoner was properly handcuffed, which this suspect was.

After rolling down the back windows just enough to let air circulate through the truck, Officer Webber secured the prisoner in the cage of his truck.

"Let's go for a hike," Deputy McMillan said.

170

As Kevin followed him through the woods, Brice explained how he was getting ready to fire up his chainsaw when he heard the dogs. He explained how he had snuck up on the poacher, catching him at the bear with a rifle and five hunting hounds.

As the two men came to the dead bear, Kevin just turned to Brice and gave a hearty high-five.

"Dude, talk about catching someone red-handed. Awesome job, Brice." Kevin went on, "Did he say what made him come up here and kill a giant bear during the closed season and with dogs? This just doesn't happen."

"The only thing to come out of his mouth is how he is a "brother in arms" and how I should give him a break," Brice answered.

"What does he mean, brother in arms?"

"He's a corrections officer at the Walla Walla penitentiary."

"You mean he was a corrections officer. I doubt he will have a job after this," Kevin noted.

"Yeah, that's the only thing he seems to be concerned about right now."

"Well, that will certainly work in our favor."

Brice reached into his right-front pants pocket and pulled out four live 30-30 cartridges and one spent shell casing. He handed them to Kevin.

"I took these out of his rifle," Brice told Kevin.

171

"You covered all the bases. You didn't leave me with much to do. Hey, if you want to get out of here, I'm good here, and Jeff (Deputy Jeff Palmer) should be here any minute," Kevin told Brice.

"No way I'm going anywhere until this done."

"Well, I sure as hell owe you one now," Kevin said.

"Yes, you do," Brice responded.

Back at the truck, Kevin opened the cage door and instructed the prisoner to step out.

"Okay, I am going to move your cuffs to the front now, but any screwing around at all and they go back behind you. And you go immediately to jail. Clear?" Kevin asked Gregg.

"Got it," Gregg responded.

After switching the cuffs to the front, a move Kevin did solely so the suspect could sign the written statement Kevin hoped would be coming soon, Kevin opened the front passenger door and told Gregg to have a seat.

With the suspect in the passenger seat and his door open, Kevin sat in the driver's seat while Brice stood adjacent to the open passenger door.

"I understand Deputy McMillan read your Miranda warnings to you and that you understood your rights, and you were still willing to talk to us. Is that correct?"

"Yes, it is," Gregg answered.

172

"This form is a waiver of your rights. If you understand your rights and are freely and voluntarily waiving your rights, I will need you to sign here and here," Kevin said as he pointed to the signature lines.

After the suspect had signed both lines, Kevin asked, "So you want to explain to me what's going on here and why you decided to kill a bear today?"

"I will answer your questions all you want, but I want full immunity in writing first," Gregg insisted.

"Well, that's not going to happen, so I guess we are done here," Kevin responded as he made a show of putting the forms away.

"If you think you're in a position to put demands on us, I think you don't fully grasp the situation here. No matter what you say or don't say, you are still going to jail today, and I am seizing your truck, your equipment, and your dogs," Kevin went on. "The only question you should ask yourself right now is; do you want me to tell the prosecutor you were fully cooperative, or do you want me to tell him you were uncooperative and without remorse?" Kevin explained.

"I will cooperate. Just tell me what you want," Gregg replied as his lower lip began to quiver.

"Okay, then back to my original question. Why?"

"Simple. I need the money. Corrections doesn't pay shit, and my wife is on disability from a back injury. We just can't seem to get our heads above water," Gregg answered.

173

"So, how does doing this help your financial situation?" Kevin asked.

"The gallbladder. I get $1.25 a gram for the gall. The gall on that bear is probably worth $400 to $500."

"Who do you sell to?" Kevin asked.

"A guy named Mike. I don't know his last name."

"So, where is this, Mike?"

"I have no idea where he lives or anything about him," Gregg answered.

"So, this is you being fully cooperative?" Kevin asked. "I sell to a guy named Mike, with no last name, no location, no anything. So how do you get the gall to Mike?"

"I call him."

"Now we're making progress. So, what's Mike's phone number?" Asked Kevin.

"I don't know, but it's on the cell phone he gave me."

"And where's that cell phone?"

"In in my glovebox. It's the blue LG."

"Do we have your permission to recover that cell phone from your glovebox?" Kevin asked.

"Yes, you do."

Brice went forward and recovered the cell phone, a light blue LG Rebel FlashFone, and brought it to Kevin.

Kevin looked over the phone and then handed it to the suspect.

"Call him and tell him you scored, and ask when you can meet with him, but no sooner than two days from now," Kevin instructed Gregg.

"Okay."

With shaking hands, Gregg scrolled to the only contact in his contacts list and pushed the phone symbol.

"Put it on speaker," Kevin ordered.

"Hey, what's up, my man?" said the voice on the other end.

"Hey, I just killed a monster, and the gallbladder is like 350 to 400 grams. It's huge. I gotta work tomorrow and Wednesday, but after that, I'm open," Gregg told Mike.

"Right on. I will get back to you tonight and work out a time."

"Sounds good. Talk to you later," Gregg answered.

"Thanks for the call," replied Mystery Mike.

"Okay. He will call back this afternoon with the time and place," Gregg informed the officers.

"You better hope so," Kevin said as he put the suspect's cell phone in his console box.

175

As Kevin began making arrangements for the bear meat to be salvaged for charity, Deputy Jeff Palmer arrived to transport the prisoner.

"Thanks, Jeff. I will be at the office in a couple of hours and will fill out the P.C. (probable cause) statement," Kevin said.

"Hey, no problem. We will take good care of him for you," Palmer replied with a smile on his face.

As Palmer drove away with the prisoner, Brice turned to Kevin and asked, "How about a ride back to my truck?"

On the way to Brice's truck, Kevin asked, "Are you off tomorrow too?"

"Yeah, today is the second of my five days off. Why?"

"I hate owing someone, so tomorrow we will cut one hell of a lot of firewood for you," Kevin answered. "What time do you want me up here?"

"You don't have to do that. But since you offered, I will meet you at 7:00, where my truck is now."

"You've got it. See you in the morning, and thanks again!" said Kevin as he dropped Brice at his truck.

Kevin then worked his way back to the suspect's vehicle, where he called for a tow truck to impound the Toyota.

As he was waiting for the wildlife salvage guys (a group of civilians who volunteered to gut, pack, cut, and wrap abandoned or

176

seized wildlife for the family shelter), Kevin called his sergeant to bring him up to speed.

After Kevin had explained the situation to Sgt. Cooper, his sergeant, told Kevin about the request for information on bear poaching. He had received the request from Sgt. Sean Dresken up north and suggested Kevin contact Dresken directly to bring him up to speed.

"What are you going to do with the dogs?" Cooper asked.

"When I get off the phone, I will take all of the dogs out on leads, and then I'll slide the box from his truck to mine. I'll load them back in the box, and after that, they will go to the animal shelter," Kevin answered.

"Last question: what about when "Mike" calls back this afternoon?"

"I have the phone, and when he calls back, I will let it go to voicemail. I'll then go down to the jail and take our boy into the interrogation room to call back," Kevin said.

"Sounds like you have thought of everything."

"There are two more things," Kevin said.

"As you now know, I didn't make this case. Deputy Brice McMillan did, and I think it would be pretty cool if our chief would send him an attaboy letter cc'd to the Sheriff," Kevin went on.

177

"That shouldn't be a problem. The chief is good at recognizing outstanding work. I will get on it today," Cooper replied. "But you said two things. What's the second?"

"I need to take tomorrow off. I gotta go cut some firewood."

"You've got it. Great job to both of you on this one."

CHAPTER 28

The Rainman noticed the call was from a new cell number. It was from one of the phones he had given to Mike months ago. *This can't be good*, Rainman thought.

"Get tired of your other phone?" Rainman asked.

"I wish. This morning I got the brush-off signal from one of my guys down in Walla Walla," Mike answered.

"Any concerns?"

"No, he doesn't know anything about us. He thinks I'm from Wenatchee, and that's all he knows."

"Well, too bad, so sad for him. Thanks for the head's up," Rainman said.

CHAPTER 29

At four p.m. Lisa called to tell Clay she was on the way and should be there by 4:45 at the latest.

While Clay was waiting, he checked his department email and found another treat from Sean. Sean had received information from the Sergeant in Walla Walla that Officer Kevin Webber had just arrested a corrections officer who had been caught right after shooting a bear that his hounds had treed. Sean had attached Webber's probable cause statement, which Clay opened next.

When Clay read the suspect had confessed to not only killing the bear but to illegal trafficking in bear gallbladder, he realized this might be the break they had been waiting for. As he read further, he came to the part about the LG Rebel FlashFone, and it seemed like something he had heard about recently. He sat back in his chair and concentrated, but it wasn't coming to him. As a last-ditch, Clay went to the documents file on his department laptop and typed "FlashFone" into the "Search Documents" box. Immediately the case report from Lisa's old detachment came up. Clay then typed FlashFone in the "find" box, and there it was. Lee K. Benson, the poacher arrested at the bear bait by the region four officers, also had an LG Rebel FlashFone.

Officer Kevin Webber's probable cause statement did not say anything about the contact numbers in the FlashFone, nor did Officer Edward's report.

Clay opened a new email and addressed it to Webber and Edwards.

180

Gentlemen: In reading the reports you both submitted on bear gall traffickers you each caught, you both refer to the suspects having in their possession LG Rebel FlashFones. I need the contact names and numbers from those phones, so if you have that information, or you can get it for us, we would greatly appreciate it. Thanks, and congratulations to both of you for outstanding cases! Clay.

When Lisa arrived, Clay asked her if she had a chance to read the P.C. statement that Sean had sent them.

"Not yet, why?"

"Kevin Webber, the officer down in Columbia County, arrested a guy yesterday who was hunting with hounds when he shot a bear during the closed season. He got caught in the act by an off-duty deputy," Clay explained.

"Awesome," Lisa replied.

"That's not the best part. The guy admitted to selling gallbladder, and he then even called and left a message for his buyer at Webber's request. But the best part is the suspect had the same cell phone make and model that the poacher your old detachment caught had on him. I just wrote both lead officers back and asked if they had the contact lists from those phones," Clay explained.

"Did the suspect give up the name of his buyer?"

"Oh yeah, that will help us a lot. The guy's name is Mike. The suspect claims he doesn't know Mike's last name or where he lives."

"Well, let's hope the guys have the contact lists from those phones," Lisa added.

181

Lisa drove to Moe's driveway gate, punched in the code, and continued up the hill to his shop. As normal, Moe was not home, but Garma and the girls rushed out to greet them.

"We are getting this truck out of your way for a while," Clay told Garma.

"Doesn't bother us any. Moe has enough room in that shop to park a 747 in there," Garma responded.

"Well, thank you very much for letting us use your shop," Lisa added.

"Our pleasure. Moe gets his law enforcement fix just being around you two. It's good for him to be involved," Garma responded.

"Sorry girls, we have to get going, but we will see you soon," Lisa said to Shenden and Chesa while giving them hugs.

As Clay got in the unmarked truck, he told Lisa, "Okay, let's leave your truck at my house so we don't bother them when we come back."

"You first."

Soon Lisa and Clay were heading up to pick up the cameras and scan the photos. Clay wanted to start with the camera on the 2320 road. As Lisa drove from camera to camera, Clay went through the familiar task of downloading and reviewing all of the photos. To his surprise, not one vehicle had gone down the 2320, but several of the other cameras had photos of various vehicles.

182

When Lisa and Clay had retrieved and downloaded all seven cameras, including Clay's personal camera, Clay found three photos of their favorite taxidermist driving around. Clay also recognized several of his "past customers" (people he had arrested for poaching in the past). Still, nothing stood out as obvious, and there certainly seemed to be no pattern to the travel of any of the vehicles.

It seemed obvious to Clay that the taxidermist was meeting people in the woods because there was never much time between the photos of him driving inbound and the photos of him driving outbound. But what exactly he was up to remained a mystery to the wardens.

Clay and Lisa had previously decided that before they put the cameras up in Lisa's area, they would drop her work truck off at her house. When they were about halfway to Lisa's house, Clay shouted, "Yes, finally a frigging break!"

"What's up?" Lisa asked.

"I'm reading an email to us from your buddy Zach Edwards. Are you ready?"

"Lay it on me," Lisa answered

"Here's the entire text of his email," Clay said as he read the email.

> Only one contact and number in the phone: Mike (509) 555-8799. I hope that helps.

"Oh wow. All we need now is to find a connection between these phones, this phone number, and anything current," Lisa said.

183

"The guy they just arrested down in the Blue Mountains might be the key, but I haven't heard back from Kevin Webber yet," Clay replied.

"So, let's just call him," Lisa said as she looked up his phone number from the department roster. "Got it!"

"Kevin. Lisa Bennington."

"Hey, Lisa. What's up?" Kevin answered.

"We are sitting here with our fingers crossed, hoping you can make our day for us. On the guy you just caught with the bear closed season, do you happen to have the number for the mystery Mike he called?"

"Yeah, but I thought I put it in the P.C. statement my sergeant sent to your sarge."

"I'm looking at it right now, and I don't see a phone number on here anywhere," Lisa responded.

"Okay, I will take a look. Can you give me about ten minutes, and I will call you back?"

"You bet. We will be waiting," Lisa answered as she hung up.

"Sounds like he has the number somewhere. He will find it," Clay said.

"Aren't you just a ray of sunshine today?"

"That's me. Always upbeat and positive," Clay replied.

184

Six minutes after they had hung up with Kevin, he called back.

Lisa literally had her fingers crossed as she answered.

"Only one contact in the entire phone: Mike at (509) 555-8799."

"You are now officially our hero!" Lisa said. "Hey, would you please write that up in a report, sign it, and send up a copy?"

"I will have it to you in an hour. Sorry about not giving it to you earlier. My bad," Kevin said.

"Don't worry about it. You may have just cracked our entire gallbladder poaching case. You're the man. Thanks again," Lisa replied.

"Any time. Glad I could help. Take care."

"So, what do you think? Will that get us a warrant?" Lisa asked.

"It should. I can't see why not. We can show that two different suspects, in two different parts of the state, were poaching and trafficking in bear gall. We can also show both suspects had identical LG Rebel FlashFones, and both phones had only one contact name and number, and it was the same for both of them," Clay said. "That really should do it for us."

"Awesome!"

"I will bet anything you want to bet, right now, that Mystery Mike turns out to be taxidermist Matt," Clay added.

"I don't think I want the opposite side of that bet. I'll pass, thanks," Lisa replied. "But I will grab his driver's license photo and send it to both of our phones, so we have the photo to show people."

After Lisa parked her patrol vehicle, she jumped in the unmarked truck with Clay.

"All right, let's go put up some cameras," Clay said.

"I'm going to shoot Sean an email, updating him on where we are now," Lisa said.

"Why?"

"To keep you from getting a lecture about not keeping him in the loop," Lisa replied. "You do know, he's not the enemy, right?"

"I know he's a pain in the ass. That's what I know about the boy."

186

CHAPTER 30

Detective David Carpenter's shift started at ten p.m. Before wading through his email, David always checked his snail-mail box in the squad room first. As he was sorting through the trial notices and subpoenas, he noticed a letter from the state patrol crime lab. This had to be about the Jane Doe dead body they found up at the Clear Creek Pit.

The death had been ruled an accidental overdose of heroin and fentanyl, but as far as David knew, the body was not yet identified.

David opened the crime lab envelope and read the single-page report, which identified the blood as being from a black bear and identified the fingerprints found on the duct tape as belonging to Hamill, Blake Eugene, with a D.O.B. of 06-24-93.

Detective Carpenter was familiar with Blake and, in fact, saw him around town all the time. *It shouldn't be too hard to find the little turd*, he thought.

Carpenter remembered, not that far back, reading a message from the Sheriff about black bear poaching. David opened his email and scrolled down until he found the message, which pretty simply stated that if he had any information involving bears, to call Clay or Lisa. The black bear blood thing was weird, and he had no idea how it could help their case, but he might as well tell them about it.

David had just seen Emily walk back toward the copier, so he poked his head around the corner and said, "Hey Em, I need to call

Lisa about a case I'm working where I found some bear blood on a tarp the victim was rolled up in. What's her cell number?"

"Was that the young woman they found up Clear Creek?" Emily asked.

"One and the same. An OD that someone didn't want to screw up their party, so they dumped her like garbage. Got some prints off the tape used to wrap her up, and they came back to Blake Hamill, one of our low-life junkies," David answered.

"I know Hamill. I see him all the time driving around in that piece of crap red Nissan truck. What have you got on him?" Emily asked.

"Need to bring him in for questioning on the "Removal or concealment of a body" crime which I'm pretty sure he did."

"Hand me your phone, and I will dial Lisa for ya," Emily said.

After David got off the phone with Lisa, he told Emily, "Lisa would like to be present when we interrogate Hamill. She said she won't say a word until after we are done with the interrogation on the body. I told her we would call as soon as we scoop up that piece of crap."

"I'll bet we can find him in less than an hour," Emily said.

"Well, let's go find the boy."

Emily and David went in different directions, in different vehicles, both in an informal race to see who could find Hamill first.

Sometimes things just work out. No more than 15 minutes after they had left the office, Emily heard David call out the stop of Hamill's truck.

Since Hamill hadn't been drinking and was only a suspect at that time, Detective Carpenter asked Hamill to drive to the Sheriff's office so they could "talk." Hamill asked a half-dozen times what this was all about. David said he would explain it at the office.

Emily called Lisa and told her they found Hamill and were bringing him to the office. Lisa said she and Clay were en route.

Before allowing Hamill inside the Sheriff's office, Detective Carpenter patted him down for weapons—finding none.

Emily caught up to David just as he walked Hamill into one of the interview rooms.

"Mr. Hamill, this is Deputy Emily Bennington, who I am pretty sure you have already met," David said.

"I know you are wondering what's happening here, but I need to read you your rights," Emily said.

After having his Miranda warnings read to him, Hamill signed an acknowledgment and waiver of Miranda.

"Yeah, but I still don't know what this is all about. I haven't done nothing," Hamill said with a whine.

"Well, what I first want to talk to you about is the body of a young woman we found wrapped in a tarp at the Clear Creek Pit," David said.

189

"Yeah, I heard about that. So, what's that got to do with me?"

"Have you ever been to the Clear Creek Pit?" David asked.

"Yeah, everyone has. That's where we used to party in high school."

"I'm talking a little more recently than that. When was the last time you were up there?"

"Oh hell, it's probably been a couple of years. I've driven by it but don't have any reason to go in there no more," Hamill said in a very shaky voice.

"Okay," David said.

"So, what do you know about this?" David continued while he turned his laptop screen toward Hamill, so he could see the photo of the dead body wrapped in the blue tarp as it was lying in the pit.

"Nothing. Is that the dead girl wrapped up in that?" Hamill asked.

"I'm pretty damned sure you know what's in that blue tarp because you are the one who wrapped her up in it."

"No way, man. No fucking way. Don't try to pin this shit on me. I'm innocent."

"Well, that's not what this report says," David said as he slid a copy of the crime lab report to Hamill.

"Your prints were all over the inside wraps of tape. So, the only question we have is; did you murder her, or was this an accident?"

190

Clay and Lisa arrived just when it was getting good and watched on the closed-circuit television until their turn.

Emily knew Hamill was toast when she first noticed a tear running down his face.

"I loved her, man. I would never do anything to hurt her. She was already dead when I found her," Hamill blubbered.

"Okay then, let's start from the very beginning. How do you know her?" David asked.

"She's my girlfriend. We were gonna get married. Then she died. Everything is all screwed up now."

"What name do you know her by?" David asked.

"Everyone just calls her Cricket, but her real name is Jessica Susan Tiller."

"Okay, so what happened?"

"Cricket had a real bad heroin habit, and I was helping her get clean. Then one day, I came home and found her dead in bed. You know, I like didn't know what to do. I know that if someone dies from drugs in your house, everyone in the house gets arrested, so I just panicked, man. So, I took care of her."

"You mean you took care of her by wrapping her in a tarp and dumping her body in a gravel pit. Is that about right?"

"Yeah, but you make it sound like I treated her like garbage. I was real careful with her. I loved her," Hamill repeated.

191

"Did you ever think of calling 911 or taking her to the hospital?"

"No, I didn't want to get in trouble."

"So, how did you know she was dead?" David asked.

"I checked for a pulse."

"Where did you get the tarp you wrapped her in?"

"It's mine. I got it out of the back of my truck."

Detective Carpenter then reduced Hamill's statement to writing, which Hamill signed after having it read back to him. Once David was done with the questions on the body dumping, Clay and Lisa walked into the already crowded room.

"You have been advised of your rights. Is that correct, Mr. Hamill?" Lisa asked.

"Yeah. She read them to me."

"Are you willing to talk to us now?" Lisa asked.

"I guess."

"Pick that crime lab report back up and read the last two lines."

"Yeah, so what?"

"So, where did the bear's blood and hair come from?"

"I guess it must be from a bear I killed last hunting season."

192

"Is that right? The problem I have is that you haven't had a fishing license since 2011, and you have never had a hunting license," Lisa explained.

"Are you a liar, Blake? Were you lying to Detective Carpenter when you told him Cricket's death was an accident?" Lisa asked.

"What? No way. No, I was telling the truth. She was already dead when I found her."

"Well, the problem I have with your credibility is you're lying to us now," Clay added. "The bear hair and blood didn't last on a tarp in the back of your truck for almost a year. It was fresh. We took tissue samples from every bear that has been poached in the last year, and I will bet the DNA from one of those samples will match the blood on your tarp. So quit bullshitting us if you want our support."

"I can't say nothing. They will kill me."

"You really think someone would kill you over a black bear?" Lisa asked.

"I know they would, but it's not just about a black bear," Hamill said in almost a whisper.

"Okay, last chance to come clean. What's the deal on the bear?" Lisa asked.

"It wasn't for me. It was for Cricket," Hamill answered, "Cricket had a real bad habit, and like I said, I was helping her, you know, and anyway, I had to get her a little H just to keep her alive while I worked her off of it."

193

What a noble boyfriend, Lisa thought.

"So, I was like complaining to a buddy of mine about not having enough money to score Cricket some H, and this buddy told me about a guy who will pay you for the gallbladder from bears. I guess the Chinese use it as an aphrodisiac or something. So, my buddy put me in touch with this guy, and he says I can get paid in cash, crystal meth, or H—my choice. So, I took the H for Cricket," Hamill said.

"Who's your buddy?" Lisa asked.

"Devon. I can't remember his last name. He lives down by four corners."

"Devon Stanfield?" Detective Carpenter asked.

"Yeah, that's him," Blake acknowledged.

"Okay, who do you sell your gallbladder to?" Lisa asked.

"A guy named Mike, but I don't know his real name."

"We need a little more than that. Where is he from? What does he look like? What's he drive? Where do you meet him? That kind of stuff."

"I have no idea where he's from, but it always takes him like three or four hours to get here when I call him. He's not huge, but he's one bad-ass looking dude, but clean-cut and short hair. He drives a whole bunch of different rigs. Sometimes trucks and sometimes cars. He tells me where to meet him and what time, but it's always around Omak somewhere. He's not like in your face or anything, but he's made it pretty clear they won't put up with snitches. He said the

194

Rainman enjoys eliminating problems, and that's just like he said it. Eliminating problems."

"Is this Mike?" Lisa asked as she held her phone up so Blake could see the photo of Matt.

"I don't think so, but I'm not sure," Blake answered.

"Who is the Rainman?" Clay asked.

"I have no idea, other than Mike said he's the big boss and not a guy to screw around with."

"You said you call Mike. So how do you call him? What's his number?" Lisa asked.

"He gave me a phone a long time ago. That's the only way I can get ahold of him. If I call by another cell, he won't answer. He said if I lost the phone, I would never hear from him again. He even told me what to say if the cops were making me talk to him. I am just supposed to say the word gallbladder, and he knows it's a set-up that way."

"Where's that phone?" Lisa asked.

"Out in my truck in the parking lot."

"Can I have your permission to retrieve it from your truck while you guys talk?" Clay asked.

"Yeah, I guess. It's in the pocket at the bottom of the door on the driver's side. It's a blue LG," Hamill answered.

"I'm gonna need your keys," Clay said as he stood.

Blake turned his car keys over to Clay, who asked Emily to accompany him to the truck as a witness.

He unlocked the driver's door, grabbed the LG Rebel FlashFone, and re-locked the truck.

When Clay walked back into the interrogation room, he waited for a pause in the conversation before asking Blake to show them the number he called to swap gallbladder for heroin.

"It's the only number in here. Mike at (509) 555-8799."

"How many bears have you killed in the last year?" Clay asked.

"Seven," Blake answered.

Lisa and Clay took the next hour getting every detail—Blake could think of—into a written statement.

After much consideration, it was decided to book Hamill for moving Cricket's body to the gravel pit while the investigations continued.

"For your safekeeping, we will book you into jail now—on the charges of moving Miss Tiller's body. We may want you to place that phone call to Mike sometime later, but we will be back in touch," Lisa told Blake.

What Lisa didn't know was that the phone, which went with the (509) 555-8799 number, had been destroyed days ago.

196

After Blake was led to jail by two jailers, Clay thanked Emily and David for their help. "You may have just given us the key to this whole case of ours. Great job you guys!"

"What do you know about getting phone records from private phone companies?" Lisa asked Clay.

"Pretty much nothing," Clay answered. "I know you need a warrant, but other than that, I've got nothing for ya."

"Well, I think that we need to have a conversation with the prosecutor tomorrow," Lisa said.

"I agree. It's getting too late to fool with the cameras tonight, so let's hold off on them until we get this phone warrant done," Clay suggested. "But I do need a ride home."

"I'll take you. I am working north tonight anyway," Emily offered. "I'm ready whenever you are."

"Sounds good," Clay responded. "I will be down here around quarter to seven tomorrow to hopefully meet with the prosecutor."

"See you in the morning," Lisa said. "There is finally a light at the end of the tunnel."

CHAPTER 31

Okanogan County Prosecutor Anthony "Tony" Breckler was a graduate of the Gonzaga University School of Law and had been a practicing attorney for twenty-three years—the last twelve of which had been with the prosecutor's office. An avid hunter and fisherman, the Spokane native, was right at home in rural Okanogan County.

While Tony prosecuted each and every case vigorously, the cases he enjoyed handling the most were wildlife cases. Tony found wildlife cases to be interesting, as well as challenging, and had always been impressed with the quality of work "his" game wardens produced. He and Clay were longtime friends who occasionally hunted and fished together.

The door to Tony's office was always open, if he wasn't having a meeting, and allowed him a sliver of a view of the reception desk. When he noticed Clay at the counter, he yelled, "We're closed. Come back never."

"Aren't you the comedian?" Clay responded.

As Tony walked toward the door, he noticed Lisa and said, "For you, I will open the shop, even though I have to admit I am disappointed in you for the company you keep."

"I've got to stick with him. Headquarters assigned me to keep him out of trouble, and it's more than a full-time job," Lisa answered.

After a robust bone-crushing handshake for Clay and a normal handshake for Lisa, he welcomed them into his office, closing the door behind them.

"To what do I owe the pleasure of your company so early in the morning?" Tony asked.

"This might take a while. Are you pressed for time?" Clay asked.

"All clear until three when I have to attend an ever so thrilling county commissioner's meeting. So, I'm all yours for the next couple of hours—until you buy me lunch, that is."

Clay and Lisa then took the next ninety minutes laying out their case, including the sworn statement of Officer Kevin Webber and his P.C. statement, the sworn report by Officer Zach Edwards and his suspect's statement, and finally, Blake Hamill's statement.

Tony asked dozens of questions to the officers as they moved through their case background.

When Clay and Lisa were done, Tony said simply, "There isn't a single judge in the land who would authorize a search warrant based on this."

Lisa's mouth dropped open in stunned astonishment. She absolutely couldn't believe it until she noticed Clay was having trouble keeping his laugh suppressed.

"Very funny. See if you get my vote next election," Lisa said.

"I think you better check the county ordinances. I believe it is unlawful for a westsider to vote in our elections until such point as that person has lived here ten years or more," Tony joked.

"Seriously, guys, this is outstanding work, and the warrant will be a piece of cake. Where you will have problems is with identifying Mike and this Rainman character," Tony explained. "You know Rainman is kind of a sissy name, like the Florist. It doesn't make me shake in my boots. It sounds more like a guy who installs lawn sprinkler systems. I am pretty sure these guys aren't Hell's Angels."

"How do you want to do this? Would you like me to draft the affidavit and warrant, or would one of you like just to have me review the one you wrote? Either way works for me," Tony asked.

"I'm totally fine with you writing it," Clay answered.

"I would like to take a stab at it first if you wouldn't mind. This will be my first warrant for a cell phone carrier, and I need to learn how to do these myself," Lisa said.

"Looks like we have identified the motivated warden in the room, haven't we, Clay?" Tony said with a smile.

"She's a little ADHD, but keep that to yourself," said Clay.

"Then Miss ADHD here might get a little frustrated at the snail's pace cell phone providers respond to subpoenas and warrants. I hope you guys aren't in a hurry. I've seen it take days or even weeks," Tony added.

"Really, not much we can do about that," added Clay.

200

"I do want to give you two something to think about. From what you have told me, there are a couple of common denominators in this case; bear gallbladder, dopers, Mike, the Rainman, and these cell phones. I know you have covered all the bases you can on the bear gallbladder side, but have you asked anyone with the drug task force about this Mike, the Rainman, or these phones?

"Since it looks like drugs are intertwined with the poaching and gallbladder trafficking, I think it might be worth checking into," Tony recommended.

"When we first started working this case hard, we contacted the troopers, the Sheriff, and the U.S. Forest Service law enforcement officers, and we brought them up to speed. But, no, we haven't updated that info at all," Lisa responded. "But we will. Thanks for that observation."

"I look forward to receiving your first draft, young lady. Just email it to me anytime. I will give you my input, which you can take or leave. Clay always ignores me and does what he wants. We will get this done and done well," Tony said as he rose to walk them to the door, "but both of you still owe me lunch."

"Thanks for the help. Lisa's wrong about you. You aren't totally worthless," Clay said, laughing while walking out the door.

Tony laughed louder and harder when he saw Lisa deliver a solid punch to Clay's left shoulder as she mouthed, "Butthead."

As Clay and Lisa walked out of the courthouse, Clay remarked, "You know he's right about updating everyone. Now we have a solid

201

link between our poaching case and dope, so we should give everyone the latest information."

"It won't take us more than an hour, so let's do it before leaving town," Lisa suggested.

"First stop should be to the Sheriff's office, especially since it's an easy walk."

Clay and Lisa took only ten minutes or so to update the Sheriff about the drug angle of their case.

"Have you run this through Spillman?" Sheriff Kevin Bryant asked.

"Nope, didn't even think about that," Clay answered.

Spillman is a law enforcement records management system, which all of the Okanogan E.M.S. (Emergency Management Services) uses, as does dispatch. The system includes all calls for service, all records, and reports, as well as a complete inventory of all property seized or held for safekeeping by law enforcement.

"Well, let's take a look right now," Sheriff Bryant said as he opened the program on his desktop computer. "There's no use in searching for suspects named Mike, but I will try Rainman.

"Nada. Let's try gall and gallbladder.

"Blanks again. Let's try the phone number. Give it to me again," Sheriff Bryant asked.

"509-555-8799," Clay said as Bryant entered it.

"Strike three. You're out," Sheriff Bryant announced.

"Try the phone itself. Enter LG Rebel FlashFone or at least LG Rebel," Lisa suggested to the Sheriff.

"Bingo! We have a winner!"

"What? What have you got?" Clay asked.

"Come around and check this out," the Sheriff said as he made room for the two officers to join him behind his desk and as he read aloud.

"Two weeks ago, Trooper Clint Greer, from right here in Omak, came upon a one-car rollover accident, with serious injuries, on Highway 73 at milepost 17. He found the driver and sole occupant to be David S. Byrd.

"It seems Mr. Byrd literally had a paper bag full of narcotics laying on top of him when Greer arrived. The bag contained 59 grams of meth and 116 grams of heroin/fentanyl mix.

"Now, take a look at the inventory of his personal property held for safe-keeping: two cell phones, a white I-phone, and a light blue LG Rebel. I believe that's what you were looking for, right?" Bryant asked with a wide smile on his face.

"I know Byrd. Hell, the tribal police have told me to watch him because he apparently is a major poacher and a pain in the butt for them," Lisa added. "So, where's Mr. Byrd and his LG Rebel right now?"

203

"He is currently a guest in our fine correctional facility, which is also where his phones are sitting."

"Clay, do you ever get tired of me saving your ass and making you look good to the bosses?" Sheriff Bryant asked.

"Nope, I'm totally fine with it, as long as you don't let it go to your already swollen head. Seriously though, this helped us a ton. Thanks," Clay said.

"Yeah, thanks, Sheriff. We appreciate it," Lisa added.

"Now, what do you want to do?" Lisa asked Clay as they walked out of the Sheriff's office.

"I think you and I need to call Greer and see if he can come in to meet with us in Breckler's office. It looks like Byrd might not only have information about our case, but it seems he is pretty well connected in the narcotics distribution angle of our case," Clay answered.

"I will call Greer if you get the prosecutor on the line, so we can see if everyone is available to meet," Lisa said.

As luck would have it, Trooper Clint Greer was in the state patrol detachment office working on paperwork when Lisa called him to invite him to a meeting with the prosecutor.

"Anything to get out of here. I'm on my way," Greer said to Lisa in response to her asking about his availability for the meeting.

"Long time no see," Tony said with a smile, "and I see you brought back-up this time. Glad you could join us, Clint."

Facing Clay and Lisa, Tony asked, "So what brings you back here so soon?"

"Your suggestion that we look at other cases to see if we could find similarities, and we found a big one," Lisa said.

"Does someone want to tell me what's going on?" Trooper Greer asked.

Lisa and Clay took the next ten minutes bringing Clint up to speed.

"So, why am I here?" asked the trooper.

"Because we will not muck around with someone else's case without involving them. We would really like to get some cooperation out of Mr. Byrd, which will likely mean making him some kind of deal on your case against him," Clay answered.

"That's all you need?" Trooper Greer asked.

"You know the max he faces on the state level is ten years— fifteen if it went federal?" Tony asked the group.

"Yep, so what could we do with him to get him to talk?" Clay asked.

"I got this one. Piece of cake. I see he has Public Defender Don Slater as his attorney. Let me make a call," Tony announced.

"Don, Tony here. Say, I have something to run past you on the David Byrd case, and I think you will want to hear it. You have a few

205

minutes to come by my office right now?" Tony said into the phone. "Great, see you soon."

"He will be here in a couple of minutes. Please let me handle this. Just sit and stare at him, like you are sick that I'm even talking to him. If you have something you just have to tell me, please ask to talk with me in the hall. I assume everyone is good with that?" Tony asked.

"You got it. Show us your magic," Clay replied.

Don Slater looked like a fifteen-year-old kid dressed in his dad's clothes as he shuffled into the room.

"Wow, I didn't know you would have backup, Tony," the public defender joked.

"Just in case you get out of control," answered Tony.

"So, what can I do for all of you?" the young lawyer asked.

"It's not what you can do for us, but what we can do for you and your client," Tony responded. "As you know, the case against your client is rock solid. There's no escape from this one. He's going to prison for a very long time."

"So, I came over so that you can tell me how easy your case will be?"

"No, you came over to hear the best and only deal your client is going to get. He has information these officers want, and in exchange for his cooperation, I am willing to make you a one-time offer, which will expire at five p.m. today."

206

"I'm listening," replied the public defender.

"Your client will plead guilty to one count of possession of a controlled substance with intent to deliver, with an agreed sentence recommendation of ten years, nothing suspended, and a $20,000 fine. This will, of course, be in exchange for his truthful and complete cooperation regarding the drug trafficking network he is a part of."

"Wow, how generous of you. You are offering my client the maximum prison sentence in exchange for his cooperation. I think it's safe to say my client will probably reject your offer, but thanks anyway," Slater said as he rose to leave.

"Oh crap. Did I forget to mention the controlled substance homicide? My bad," Tony added.

"What controlled substance homicide?"

"The death of this beautiful young woman, Jessica Tiller," Tony responded as he reached in the Jessica Tiller file and slid the autopsy photos to the public defender. "Dead at 20-years of age by the very same combination of heroin and fentanyl as was found in your client's possession. These officers are actively pursuing this case right now, and you know as well as I do, it will just be a matter of time before we connect all the dots on this. We currently have another member of their criminal enterprise in custody, and the first one to talk gets this deal. So, unless your client wants to spend the rest of his miserable life in prison, I recommend he takes the deal. It doesn't matter if Byrd sold it to Joe Smith and Smith sold it to Tiller. It's all coming down soon with or without Byrd's assistance.

"You know as well as I do, the courts do not look too favorably at people who deal in death. This is headlines kind of shit. We want the top of this organization, not a mid-level dealer, but as they say, a bird in the hand or, in this case, a Byrd in the hand."

"So, if we take this, you will grant my client full immunity on the controlled substance homicide?" Slater asked.

"As it relates to the death of Jessica Tiller only, yes, but only with complete and truthful testimony from your client. Anyone else your client killed is fair game," Tony replied.

"I will discuss it with my client and get back to you."

"Today by five p.m., and that's non-negotiable. If we don't have a deal by 5:00, he's all mine."

"Understood. Thanks, Tony," Slater said as he shook Tony's hand on his way out.

After the attorney had left, Lisa asked, "How did we connect the Tiller death to Byrd?"

"Same type of dope," Tony responded.

"Yeah, but what indicates Byrd sold that heroin to Jessica Tiller?" Lisa asked.

"I'm sorry. Did I say we had proof of that sale? It sure seems possible the dope that killed Tiller came from Byrd," Tony added.

"That was a thing of beauty," Trooper Greer said.

208

"We will see what happens, but I would recommend you two get ready to question Byrd tomorrow. When his lawyer calls me back to accept the offer, I will let you know," Tony stated.

"Thanks for the help. I will get to work on that warrant now," Lisa said. "But first, I want to pull Blake Hamill into an interrogation room to get him to make a phone call for us."

While Blake was anxious to get out of his cell, he was less than thrilled when he saw the reason why. Once the door to the interrogation room closed, Lisa asked Blake, "Are you still willing to place the phone call for us?"

"Yeah, I guess so."

"Okay, all we need you to do is tell him you have a couple for him and you would like to meet up this weekend sometime."

"Does that mean I'm getting out?"

"It's like we told you before; once you help us out a little, we will sit down and discuss the whole thing with the prosecutor. That's why we haven't charged you with all of the game violations yet. Sound good?"

"Whatever. Give me the phone. I'll make the call."

"Put the call on speaker," Lisa said as she handed Blake the phone.

"Okay, here we go," Blake said as he punched the call button on the cell phone.

"The number you have called is no longer in service. If you feel you have reached the message in error, please check the number and try again," said the recorded message.

"Another dead-end," Lisa said.

"Nah, he told us about this. He said if he ever thinks someone got caught, or if he gets the brush-off signal, he would call each one of us with his new number. Let me check voicemail," Blake said as he dialed his voicemail.

"Nothing. I don't get it. Well, maybe he'll call later," Blake added.

"Yeah, maybe. Thanks for trying," Lisa replied.

"When do I get out?"

"We will get back to you on that," Clay said as they notified the jail staff that they were ready to leave.

As they were walking out to their truck, Clay asked Lisa, "Would you do me a favor and ask Emily if Detective Carpenter called out the stop of Hamill on the radio."

"Sure."

After Lisa got off the phone, she said, "He sure did. You think that burned him because of scanners?"

"That and the fact you can look up the jail roster on the internet. I think whoever Mike is, he's careful," Clay said. "Seems like every time we take a step forward, we take two steps back."

"I sure as hell hope the deal with Byrd works out," Lisa added.

"Me too. Want to go put those cameras up now?" Clay asked.

"I better get to work on that cell phone warrant," Lisa answered. "How about in the morning? Seven tomorrow morning, same place?"

As they were driving back to Lisa's house, Clay's cell phone rang. Clay looked at the caller ID and then muted the phone.

"Who's that? The sarge?"

"It's just Moe. I will call him back on my way home," Clay said.

Clay dropped Lisa off at the back of her house before heading home himself. He called Moe back as he drove.

"My shop looks empty. Where did you take my new truck?" Moe asked.

"We took it down to Lisa's because we are having problems in her area now, so that's where we are concentrating our efforts."

"You guys making any progress?" Moe asked.

"A little, but it seems like we are hitting dead-end after dead-end. We just need a break. Hell, we may never figure this out."

"If there is anything at all I can do, just let me know," Moe said.

"Just keep an eye on the taxidermist for me. Try to get him to open up to you a little," Clay requested.

"I will try, but I'm telling you, the guy seems to me to be pretty honest, and I only talk to him about two minutes a day."

"I guess I'm just hoping it would be that easy," Clay responded.

"Hey, I was calling to see if you want to hit Crooked Creek tomorrow? I was up there today and creamed them. Got a couple of rainbows over fourteen inches," Moe asked.

"I can't in the morning, but tomorrow afternoon would work."

"Wanna leave about four tomorrow afternoon?" Moe asked.

"I will pick you up at four."

During the conversation, Clay's phone notified him of a new text.

"You have to work in the morning?"

"Yep, just for a few hours. I just gotta help Lisa out for a while. See you tomorrow."

"See ya then. Twenty bucks on the biggest?" Moe offered.

"I hate to keep taking your money, but you're on."

As soon as Clay hung up, he looked at the text from Tony:

"Public defender called. We've got a deal. Talk to ya tomorrow."

CHAPTER 32

Lisa quietly closed the back door so as not to wake Emily as she headed out to meet Clay in the driveway.

"Morning. Don't you look all chipper this morning? Don't tell me why. I don't want to know," Lisa remarked to Clay.

"Is your mind always in the gutter? I just have some news I think you will be pretty happy to hear."

"I'm waiting."

"Tony texted me last night, and Byrd's attorney said they will take the deal. Tony wants us to give him a call today to work out the details."

"Awesome," Lisa said as she gave Clay a fist bump, "let's go put up some cameras, and then we can call him at eight, right?"

"Yep, that will work. He's always in by eight."

Between setting up the third camera and the fourth, Clay said, "I still think the taxidermist is involved. I drive by his house and his shop basically every time I leave home, and he is gone at very strange hours. He's dirty. I want to slap one of those trackers on his truck, just to see where he goes."

"Without a warrant, that's a big no-no," Lisa warned. "Please don't go all cowboy on me. Let's play by the rules all the way."

"I didn't say I was going to put the tracker on. I said I wanted to. Just thinking out loud."

"Hey, it's time to give Tony a call. Me or you?" Lisa asked.

"Go for it. I might go all cowboy on him," Clay said.

"Easy buckaroo. I will make the call." Lisa dialed the prosecutor's office, then put it on speaker.

Once Tony was on the line, Lisa asked, "What's the deal with Mr. Byrd?"

"His attorney called yesterday, right before we closed shop. He said his client would take the deal on one condition: that he is given credit for time served. Since we are only talking about a couple of weeks off a ten-year sentence, I was good with it. He had to get something for his client, so it looks like he actually did something for him."

"You can interview him today if you want. His attorney insists on being present, so I will be there too. Whenever you two are ready, let me know, and I will set it up," Tony said.

"That's awesome. We are ready whenever you can set it up. The earlier, the better," Lisa said as she looked to see if Clay agreed.

Clay gave Lisa the thumbs up.

"All right. I will call you back when I have it all set. Great job, guys."

"I don't know if you have checked your email yet, but I have my first draft of the affidavit and search warrant done, and I sent it to you last night," Lisa said.

214

"I will take a look at it, but we better hold off on it until we hear what Mr. Byrd has to say. I'm hoping his information will be useful enough to include in the affidavit too."

"Thanks. Talk to you soon," Lisa said as she ended the call.

"Well, this should shape up to be an interesting day," Clay said.

They had the last of the cameras put in place by eleven a.m. and hadn't yet heard back from Tony.

"You want to go by the detachment office and work on our reports until we hear from Tony?" Lisa asked. "I asked the Department of Licensing to send me driver's license photos of five men who were all similar in appearance, including Matt Davis, so that I could put together a proper photo montage. I just got the pics."

Clay looked over at the laptop mounted on a swivel stand and answered, "I see Super Sarge is there. I guess we can kill two birds with one stone and bring him up to speed."

"I thought you two would have a lot of catching up to do—some solid male-bonding time."

As they were driving to the office, Clay asked, "Once we are done interviewing Byrd and you get done with your search warrants, what's left on our to-do list?"

"Just monitoring the cameras and working the woods. Why, what have you got in mind?"

"I just have to see what Matt Davis is up to, so I want to use the unmarked to do some surveillance on him. I figured I would start

215

watching his house at nine or ten at night and sit there all night if I had to. I want to see what the hell he is doing in the woods and why he is keeping such strange hours," Clay answered.

"You are getting a bit obsessed with the guy, aren't you? I mean, we have nothing to tie him to any of this."

"Oh well, it won't do any harm to at least watch him for a night or two. My time isn't worth that much anyway. I will need to take the unmarked and the NVGs for a while," Clay stated.

"So, now we aren't partners?"

"No, I just know you think I'm wasting my time on him, and you're probably right," Clay responded.

"You tell me when, and I will bring the truck and NVGs, but I'm going with you. Got it?"

"Yes, ma'am."

They arrived at the WDFW Okanogan Detachment Office at 11:45.

"It's the A-team," Sean said when he saw Clay and Lisa walk through the door. "How's the investigation going?"

Clay took about fifteen minutes to update Sean, leaving out a great deal of detail. Lisa used the time to complete her photomontage, which she printed in full color.

"Sounds like you guys have been busy. Anything I can do to help?"

216

"One thing I can think of is checking back with the other regions and asking for a case report on every bear case anyone made in the last year. We need all the details, including property seized or held for safe-keeping," Lisa told Sean. "Also, did you ever hear back from B.C.?"

"I will get that request for reports out right now. As for the B.C. Conservation Officers, the guy I spoke with said he asked their officers, but nothing jumped out at them."

"We could always use help on night patrols," Clay added as he noticed Lisa giving him the look.

"I'd love to, but with the new baby at home, Angie's not getting much sleep, and she would kill me," Sean answered.

"Okay," was all Clay could come up with in response.

The officers had been working on their reports for about an hour when Tony called, "Can you guys be here in a half-hour?"

"We will be there in fifteen minutes," Clay said as he packed up his paperwork.

"Okay. We reserved the superior court jury room for our meeting. It's private, out of public view, and the jail staff can bring Byrd up the back elevator," Tony added.

"See you in a few," Clay answered.

"Hey, I also invited Dave Carpenter because of the drug aspect. Hope you don't mind?"

217

"No, that's fine. We could use his expertise. See you in a few," Clay said.

"Time for us to go. Catch ya later, Sean," Clay said as he walked out ahead of Lisa.

"Good luck, guys."

Lisa and Clay arrived at the courthouse ten minutes later and found their way up to the superior court jury room, where they noticed a jailer posted outside of the door.

Tony was sitting at one end of the long conference table, while Public Defender Don Slater sat with his client to one side, and Detective Carpenter sat at the other end, leaving the opposite side open for Clay and Lisa. Byrd was in a wheelchair and sported several bandages but seemed to be recovering well.

"Mr. Slater, Mr. Byrd, and I have gone through the agreement and conditions and are ready to go whenever you are," Tony stated before continuing. "Mr. Byrd, I think you already know Officer Lisa Bennington, and this is Officer Clay Newberry."

"Alright," Byrd responded.

"Who wants to go first?" Tony asked.

"I will," said Lisa. "I first want you to tell me where and exactly how you acquired the drugs you were found with on the day of your accident."

"I got them from Amy."

218

"This is going to take all day if you keep answering in five words or less. How about you explain things a bit—like who's Amy?" Lisa asked.

"I don't know nothing else about her. All I ever heard was Amy. Nobody uses their real names anyway."

"Where's Amy from, and what does she drive?" Clay asked.

"I don't have any idea where she's from, but she normally drives a dark blue Ford Escape."

"How much did you pay for the drugs you had that day?"

"I paid in bear gallbladder. Amy always lets me decide how I'm gonna pay—in cash or in gallbladder. She gives me a buck and a quarter for every gram of fresh or frozen gallbladder. Sometimes I don't have enough gallbladder, so I use cash, but it's pure profit if I just pay in gallbladder," Byrd answered.

"Where do you get the gallbladder?" asked Clay.

"Some are from bears I have killed on the rez, and some come from friends of mine who bring them to me."

"So, when the friends bring you gall, do you pay them in drugs too?" Lisa asked.

"Yeah, I give them a hundred-dollar credit for every gall."

"How much weight do you move a month?" Lisa asked.

"Like around a quarter pound of H and a couple of ounces of crystal. That's it."

"When do you add the fentanyl to the heroin?" Detective Carpenter asked.

"I don't touch that shit, and if anyone says I did, then they are fucking lying," Byrd responded.

"Well, the heroin was laced with it, so where did it come from?" Carpenter asked.

"I have no idea, but it wasn't me."

"How did you meet Amy?" Lisa asked.

"A native I know, who lives off-rez, told me about her. He was doing business with her, but it was small potatoes," Byrd said. "So, I met her like a year ago, and the rest is history. I'm sure I move more product than almost all of her other associates. She calls us associates."

"How do you get in touch with Amy?" Lisa asked.

"They gave me a cell phone, and I just call her on that."

"Did the phone come with Amy's number already programmed in it?" Clay asked.

"Yeah, it's the only number in my phone, and I'm not supposed to use it for anything else. She said we are even supposed to take that little plastic card out of the phone when we aren't using it."

"Have you ever dealt with anyone other than Amy?"

"Yeah, but only on the day of my accident. She just showed up out of the blue with this new guy, Mike, who she said is the big boss."

"What did he look like?"

"White guy, about 35 to 40, mean-ass looking like he would just as soon slit your throat as talk to ya. Just kinda average-sized—but mean."

"You have any way to reach Mike?" Lisa asked.

"Nope. Like I said, Amy just brought him one day."

"Have you ever heard the name of Rainman?" Lisa asked.

"Rainman? No, I never heard of Rainman. Who the hell is that supposed to be?"

"I want you to look at six photos and tell me if you recognize anyone. Take your time, don't rush, and just do your best." Lisa said as she slid her photo montage to Byrd.

Byrd took the montage, looked it over carefully, and then slowly handed it back to Lisa.

"Nope. I don't know none of them."

"Are you sure? Look again," Clay asked.

"Officer, he answered your question to the best of his abilities. I don't think badgering him will help and would likely invalidate the identification if there were one," Don Slater added.

221

Clay just stared at Slater, making the young attorney visibly nervous.

"Who else do you know that deals with Amy or Mike?" Lisa asked.

"I don't know nobody else who deals with them, which is funny because they have the best dope for the lowest price of anyone around."

"Have you ever been offered fentanyl?" Detective Carpenter asked.

"No, and I wouldn't take it. That shit kills people dead," Byrd answered.

"Did Amy or Mike ever give you any codes or rules?" Lisa asked.

"Yeah, they said if the cops ever tried to get us by making one of us call her, Amy said to go ahead and call, but I was supposed to say gallbladder right off the bat. Then they would know I am being forced to make the call. Then they would dump their phone and get me a new phone," Byrd said.

Byrd added, "Amy was always reminding me of the rule of six B's—No booze, bud, babes, butts, brass, or bragging."

"Looks like you might have forgotten that rule when you had your accident. Your blood came back positive for heroin and fentanyl," Carpenter said.

"Seriously? Those assholes gave me fentanyl too?"

"Yep, no honor among criminals, I guess," Clay added.

"Can you think of any way that we could get in with Amy and Mike?" Carpenter asked.

"Not unless your cops can use, because the first thing Amy did when we met was to give me a free line of H and tell me to snort it right in front of her."

"One last question: will you consent to the electronic search of the cell phone Amy gave you?" Lisa asked.

"Whatever, sure. Hell, you can have the phone. I won't be using it," Byrd responded.

The officers were out of questions but weren't that much further ahead than they were before talking to Byrd.

Tony looked at all three officers and asked if there were any more questions. There were not.

"Thank you, Mr. Byrd. We may have more questions for you in the future. We would instruct you to keep this conversation confidential. Nothing that was said in this room will leave this room. Understood?" Tony asked.

"Yeah, like I was going to go back down to the jail and tell everyone I just spent the afternoon ratting out my supplier. That would really help me out."

Tony stood and opened the door so that the jailer could retrieve his prisoner.

"Thank you all for coming. I hope this was fruitful. Lisa and Clay, would you mind walking with me to my office?" Tony asked.

On the walk back to his office, the prosecutor told Lisa, "I looked over your warrant affidavit and warrant, and you did an outstanding job, especially for your first one. I made some changes, and now we have more information to add, which I can take care of in half an hour or so if you have time?"

"Sure," Lisa answered.

"This doesn't fit under the exigent circumstances rules, but I certainly think that because this fentanyl-laced heroin is lethal and is being sold in our county every day, that should certainly get us an expedited return."

Another hour later, Lisa had her affidavit, the warrant itself, the warrant return, and a letter for the judge to sign asking for this return to be expedited for public safety reasons.

"You're good to go now. I suggest you run over to Judge McKinney's and see if you can catch him before the afternoon arraignment schedule," Tony said. "And, great job, guys. I mean it. This is outstanding stuff, and I have no doubt it will all come together."

"No, thank you. This is one of the things I like best about this county. In King County, we would be lucky if a deputy prosecutor would give us the time of day. I'm never leaving, and you can't either," Lisa said.

"I don't know. Will I get your vote now?"

224

"You always had it, and you know it," Lisa said with a smile. "We better get going."

"Thanks, Tony," Clay added.

Judge William McKinney had been on the bench for three decades, and it showed. If he was a hundred pounds heavier, he could be mistaken for Santa Claus, with his white hair and beard, but he certainly wasn't jolly or festive when it came to criminals. He had a reputation as a tough, no-bull, hanging judge, which certainly helped him win elections.

Judge McKinney's clerk called into the judge's chambers to inform his honor he had visitors, "Your honor, there are two game officers out here who would very much like to speak to you."

The clerk got off the phone and said, "Go on in. He's expecting you."

After handshakes, the Judge asked, "What brings you to the court today?"

"Your honor, we have a search warrant for cellular phone records we would like you to look at," Lisa requested.

"Very well, young lady, let's see what you've got here."

The judge put on a pair of reading glasses, which rested more than halfway down his nose—just like Santa.

"So, you are asking this FlashFone company to provide you with call and text records to or from one of their phones to any and all others, names and other identifying information regarding where

225

FlashFone sold these particular phones to, and records of cell towers used by these particular phones for the last two-years. Am I correct?"

"Yes, your honor," Lisa responded.

"I see you also wrote a letter for me to sign, stating that this should be expedited for public safety reasons, and you would like the court to seal the warrant and affidavit?"

"Yes, your honor. As you read in my affidavit, this fentanyl-laced heroin is still out there, and it's potentially lethal. If the word gets out about this warrant, we might lose valuable opportunities to stop all of this."

"I see you provided the phone company with three email addresses, which is fine, but I sure hope this street address isn't your home address, Miss Bennington."

"No, your honor, that is the address of our detachment office. The three email addresses are for our Sergeant and the two of us."

"Good. Good."

As Judge McKinney began signing the documents in the appropriate places, he told Lisa, "I want to say, this warrant was superb. Outstanding job, Officer Bennington."

"Thank you, your honor, but the prosecutor helped me a great deal in writing this up," Lisa responded.

"Honest and intelligent. You better look out, Clay, she's going to replace you someday."

"At this point, your honor, I wouldn't mind being replaced," Clay said. They both laughed.

"Well, you have your warrant. Now go out and catch these scourges and bring them to me."

"We will try our best, your honor," Lisa replied.

"Take these to my clerk. She will record these, assign you a warrant number, and make you as many copies as you desire. Now, if there is nothing else, I'm needed in an arraignment in ten minutes."

"That's all, your honor. Thanks for your time," Lisa said as they all three stood to leave.

The court clerk assigned a number to the warrant, stamped it, and made four copies for the officers, returning the originals to Lisa.

"Would you like me to go ahead and fax this warrant to FlashFone?" the clerk asked.

"That would be very helpful. Thank you," Lisa responded.

When the fax had been sent, the clerk handed Lisa the fax confirmation.

It was now time to hurry up and wait.

"You about ready to call it a day? I've got a date tonight," Clay told Lisa.

"Yep, let's call it. Who's the date, and where are you going?"

"The location of our date is Crooked Creek, and my date is Moe."

227

"Say hi for me. Tell him that Emily and I want to have all of you down to our place as soon as our schedules work out," Lisa said.

"Good luck," Lisa said as Clay dropped her off at her driveway.

"Thanks."

"Hey Clay, give me your word that you won't go sneaking around in the dark without me, okay?"

"You've got my word."

CHAPTER 33

"So, what did you catch them on the other day?" Clay asked Moe.

"You know, I just don't remember."

"Oh, so that's how it's going to be, huh? It doesn't matter that much because the presentation is much more important than the fly."

"Guess we will see, won't we?" Moe quipped.

"That we will," replied Clay.

"It seems like you have been working seven days a week lately. Are you making any progress?" Moe inquired.

"Slowly. We have a couple of low-level guys we have put the squeeze on, but the problem is that none of them know much. They generally only deal with one person, and they don't know anything about him or even where he lives," Clay said.

"So, how do the low-level guys find their suppliers when they need to?"

"Burner cell phones," Clay answered.

"Can't you get their phone records?"

"Yeah, why didn't we think of that?" Clay said with a chuckle, then added, "We are already on it."

The two men went their separate ways on the creek, agreeing to meet at the truck at 7:30.

Clay spent the first half-hour using a #16 Parachute Adams dry fly with very little luck, but when he switched to a #18 Beadhead Pheasant Tail nymph, he started slamming them.

As Clay was fishing, he realized just how wound up he had been about this case. He needed to do more of this. He had to leave work at work, but that's easier said than done.

Clay totally lost track of time and fished until he couldn't see his strike indicator anymore. Clay had only kept one fish, but it would certainly be the winner since he had a 17" fat Rainbow in his soft creel.

When he got back to the truck, he noticed Moe sitting on the tailgate with a beer in his hands, tapping on his watch.

Moe tossed Clay a beer and said, "Just where have you been, young man? I was worried sick."

"Yeah, the only thing you were worried about was getting your ass kicked again. Grab my $20 out of your wallet," Clay announced as he slid the trout onto the tailgate.

"Holy crap! That's huge. What did you get him on?"

"You know, I just don't remember," Clay answered.

"Well, I guess it's time to open my wallet," Moe said as he reached in the cooler for what Clay thought was another round of beers, but instead, Moe pulled out a beautiful 21" brown trout. "So I can tuck that $20 bill of yours safely away."

"You are the luckiest fool I've ever known," Clay muttered as he handed Moe a $20.

230

"Skill, my man. Nothing but skill."

The conversation on the fifteen-minute drive back to Moe's was centered around fishing. Moe suggested that Clay consider a fishing trip to Alaska for next year, which did pique Clay's interest.

As Clay was driving up Moe's driveway, Moe asked, "You got time to come in and say hi to everyone?"

"I appreciate the offer, but I haven't seen much of Karen lately, and I think I should head home. Say hi to everyone for me."

"Will do, my friend. Have a good night and catch those bastards soon so that we can get back to the important things, like fishing."

Clay drove past Matt Davis' house on his way home and noticed his truck was gone.

CHAPTER 34

Clay waited until nine a.m. before he texted Lisa, "I have a proposal. How about we both take a couple of days off, and then on Monday night, we can start surveillance on my guy up here?"

"You just won't give up on him, will you? Okay, here's my counterproposal. I will give you five days of whatever hours you want to work it. Then if it doesn't produce anything, you give up on him."

"Deal, but if it leads to anything, we stay with it?" Clay asked.

"Fair enough," Lisa replied.

"Can you pick me up at my place, in the unmarked truck, at around eight p.m. on Monday?"

"Will do. See ya then."

"And remember to bring the NVGs," Clay added.

"Duh," was Lisa's one-word response.

Clay spent the next three days catching up on honey-dos and getting some rest between the projects, but before long, Monday had arrived, and Clay found himself back in the unmarked vehicle. Both Clay and Lisa had decided to wear their full uniforms, but with a civilian jacket over the top.

"Where to?" Lisa asked once Clay was buckled in.

"I found a spot one block over from his house, on 18th by the equipment shed for the baseball field, where we can park and see his truck, but he won't be able to make us."

Lisa pulled the truck into the hidey-hole Clay had found and then shut down the truck. "How long do you want to sit here?" Lisa asked.

"Until first light at around 6:30. One of us can sleep while the other keeps watch. So just tell me if at any time you feel like taking a nap," Clay instructed.

"I kinda feel like an idiot sitting in town watching one guy's pickup."

"Okay, I have a better idea. Around eleven tonight, I will sneak over and stick a tracker on the underside of his truck, and then we won't have to sit here. But you wanted to play by all the rules, so here we sit."

Time passed very slowly while the two officers sat watching a parked truck all night.

Nothing happened at all the first two nights. The truck didn't move, and Matt Davis didn't have a single visitor. They knew Matt was home because they could see the glow of his television set dancing around on the curtains.

Finally, on Wednesday at 10:15 p.m., the two officers had some excitement as they followed Matt Davis from his house to Moe-Mart, where they watched him walk out with a 12-pack of beer.

233

CHAPTER 35

Friday morning, at about 4:15 a.m., Clay was just about asleep when Lisa got his instant attention. "Hey, we have movement," she said while scanning through her binoculars. Clay sat straight up and, using his binos, verified it was indeed Matt Davis.

Lisa activated the NVGs and slipped them on her head while they waited for the silver Toyota's headlights to come on. Finally, the lights came on, and the truck began to move. Once the Toyota started rolling, Lisa fired up their vehicle and started to follow just as they had practiced, except that the unmarked truck did not have cut-out switches. To avoid emitting brake lights, Lisa had to slow down and stop the truck by depressing the parking brake, then releasing it to go faster.

Being the bustling nightlife capital of the world, there wasn't another car in sight, so Lisa had no trouble following the glow of Matt's headlights. The Toyota first turned on Cherry Street and then turned north on Eastlake Road, driving by the airport. Clay began to think Matt was just heading to someone's house until he turned left on Eder Road. Clay knew Eder Road first meandered through several apple orchards before it moved into the rolling hills northeast of town.

Lisa followed far enough back that there was no way Matt could have seen them. Finally, after traveling about seven miles, Lisa saw the truck turn back to the west onto some D.N.R. state ground. She felt her pulse begin to quicken as she knew this was not normal.

"You see that? He just turned. So, what's up that road?" Lisa asked.

"You have a slight advantage over me when it comes to seeing land features," Clay reminded Lisa, "so I will wait to see where he turned before answering that one."

Lisa reached the spot where she believed he had turned, but she could no longer see his truck.

"I'll check it out," Clay said as he exited the vehicle at the intersection of the Eder Road and the dirt two-track road to the left.

Clay knelt on the dirt side road and shined his flashlight sideways, parallel to the road.

"This is definitely it, which I don't get," Clay said as he climbed back in. "I know this road, and it's rough and only goes a mile or so before it just dead ends. Let's just go a little further up the hill and then walk the rest of the way to check it out."

"Pull into the next spot you think goes far enough into the trees to hide our truck," Clay instructed Lisa.

Within a few short minutes, Lisa pulled through a small opening in the trees and dropped down toward a dry creek bed. They cut the engine and listened. Nothing at all. It was totally quiet, and there was no sign of lights.

"Want to go see what he's up to?" Clay asked as he chambered a round in his department-issued AR-15.

235

"Let's do it. But I've got to tell radio where we are," Lisa said. Lisa then advised radio, by cell phone, of their location and advised them they would be away from the vehicle for a while.

Seeing Clay shoulder his defensive rifle made it very real for Lisa. If Clay were correct, and Matt was their man, they could very well be walking into something very serious. Lisa looked at Clay and instantly wished she could stay as calm as he did. At least outwardly, Clay looked like this was a routine contact and nothing more. *Nerves of steel,* Lisa thought.

Both officers exited the truck and started walking—with Lisa wearing the night vision goggles and Clay walking behind her with his left hand on her right shoulder for guidance. The AR-15 was slung over his right shoulder. As the officers crested the hill, Lisa could see a faint light, about 700 yards away, but couldn't make out anything else.

Even though the night was warm, Clay felt a cold shiver. His stomach was in knots, and he was so nervous that he could hardly breathe. He felt embarrassed and even ashamed when he noticed Lisa was alert but totally calm. *I'm getting too old for this shit,* Clay thought.

"Find us a way to get down there without being seen or heard," Clay whispered to Lisa.

"Follow me," she answered as she continued the hike.

Progress was slow as Lisa picked her steps very carefully. Knowing Clay couldn't even see his own feet in the dark, it was up to her to pick a path along the rugged road, which minimized the chance of stepping on sticks or tripping on rocks.

At a distance, which she guessed to be about 200 yards, Lisa came to a stop and whispered to Clay, "He's right there, but I have no idea what he's doing."

Clay scanned the scene with his binos, but he couldn't make out much detail in the dark. "It looks like another truck is there too. I see the right corner of the back of another pickup. He's meeting someone. Can I take a look with the NVGs for a sec?"

"Sure," Lisa said as she removed the goggles.

After a short walk, Clay returned to Lisa and handed the NVGs to her.

"Not much to add. It looks like two trucks are there. One is Matt's, but I can't see much of the second one. It looks like two guys standing by Matt's truck. Let's go join the party and see what the hell is going on here," Clay whispered.

With that, Lisa took up the lead again, with Clay's left hand on her right shoulder. Lisa carefully guided them down the hill to the meeting. The closer they got, the louder the voices were. Then they could hear laughing from the men below them.

Lisa and Clay were within 50 yards of Matt and the other man when they heard a strange sound, a whirling/buzzing sound neither of them recognized, and it was getting louder. Lisa continued guiding Clay toward the men who were standing in a small opening in the dark.

237

"Come to papa," she heard one of the men say as the source of the whirling sound got closer. Lisa watched as both men slid latex gloves over their hands.

"It's a drone," Lisa whispered to Clay as they watched a six-bladed drone come to a gentle landing in the opening.

The shorter of the two men switched on a powerful headlamp he was wearing under the hood of his sweatshirt, bathing the drone in LED light. The same man picked the drone up and carried it to the tailgate of Matt's Toyota, where he turned it over, exposing a container strapped to the underside. Both men then opened the container and dumped cellophane-wrapped packages out. Clay had seen enough.

Now, only 30 wide-open yards from the men, Lisa saw Clay bring the AR-15 to his shoulder. She then flipped her NVGs up, bringing her flashlight and Glock pistol to the ready position. Lisa and Clay continued to creep along until they got to within fifteen yards of the men, still without being noticed.

"POLICE. HANDS ON TOP OF YOUR HEADS, PALMS UP. TURN AWAY AND KNEEL DOWN!" Lisa commanded as both officers trained their flashlights and firearms on the men.

Matt immediately placed his hands palms up on his head, turned away, knelt, and surrendered, while the hoodie man remained frozen with his back turned to the officers.

"Now, asshole. Hands up now!" Clay shouted.

Slowly and deliberately, the second suspect raised his left hand, but he kept his right hand in front of him and out of sight, with his back turned to the officers.

"Don't do it. Don't fucking do it," Matt yelled to his partner in crime.

Clay's heart felt as if it would burst out of his chest. For Clay, time had slowed to a crawl. The next few seconds were in slow motion in his perception. Almost simultaneously, Matt, from a kneeling position, yelled, "Gun!" as the second suspect turned his head toward the officers.

As the second suspect's right hand came up and around with a pistol on the same horizontal plane as Lisa's head, both officers clearly saw the gun in Moe's right hand. But, only Lisa reacted. The barking of Lisa's pistol was almost deafening as her Glock 21 45 ACP sent two rounds into Moe's chest.

Clay remained motionless—his AR pointed toward the ground and a look of horror on his face.

"Clay! Clay! Hey, wake up man. I need help!" Lisa screamed at Clay, "Come on. Cover me!"

Without a word, Clay slowly walked over to Moe, laying on his back and struggling to breathe. Clay bent over, picked Moe's gun up, and shoved it in his duty belt behind his back.

Clay rested the muzzle of his rifle in the center of Moe's forehead as he spoke quietly, "You piece of shit. You were going to shoot us, huh? The only reason I'm not putting one in your fucking head right

239

now is because it would be too easy for you. You can bleed out here or die in prison. I don't give a shit either way."

"I'll cuff them if you will cover me," Lisa told Clay, who she noticed had tears streaming down his face.

"Okay, I've got you, partner," Clay responded in a wavering voice while stepping back, so he could effectively cover both men.

Before Lisa went forward to cuff the suspects, she advised radio of the shooting, requested medical assistance and backup, and provided their exact location.

Lisa first wanted to contain the uninjured bad guy, so she cuffed and searched Matt Davis since, at that time, he was the greater threat. Matt had no weapons of any kind—just two cell phones and a set of keys.

After Matt was cuffed and searched, Lisa instructed him, "Kneel, cross your feet, and now sit back on your feet." Matt complied without saying a word.

Lisa then moved over to Moe, who was still conscious and trying to speak. Lisa didn't see any practical way to handcuff Moe behind his back due to his injuries, so she cuffed his wrists together in front.

Moe repeatedly begged, "Let me die. Let me die," as Lisa searched him very thoroughly, especially the areas of his body he could still reach. He was all clear.

After both men were secured, Lisa asked Clay to walk back and get their truck. Before Clay left the scene, Lisa looked in and around both of the suspects' vehicles for anything or anyone they may have missed. Twelve minutes later, Clay was backing down the hill to the opening, stopping short of the "crime scene."

"Do not move an inch," Lisa ordered Matt.

After taking care of Matt Davis, she retrieved her trauma kit from her pack. Kneeling next to Moe, Lisa told him, "Okay, I'm just going to check you out and see if I can help you a little." To this, Moe responded by shaking his head, "no."

Lisa first cut open Moe's sweatshirt, revealing two bullet holes within 3" of each other and just right of his sternum halfway to the bottom of his ribcage. Lisa removed a QuikClot sponge and a wide roll of medical tape from her kit. The bullet wounds were so close to each other that one sponge covered both holes. Lisa taped the sponge in place and then asked Clay to help her roll Moe onto his right side, "So he won't drown in his own blood."

Lisa could hear sirens approaching as they were getting positioned to roll Moe on his side. As Clay reached over Moe's body to get a grip on Moe's left side, Lisa heard Clay whisper to Moe, "You owe her your life, asshole, because if it was just me, I'm pretty sure you wouldn't have made it this long. I'm still hoping you won't."

As both officers stood to direct the responding units in, Clay spoke softly to Lisa, "You saved my life. No doubt about it, you saved my life because I had my head so far up my ass, I couldn't see it," Clay said with a shaky voice. "Thank you.

241

"Lisa, I promise you, I didn't know any of this, and I sure didn't have anything to do with it. It's important to me that you believe me," Clay continued.

"Not for a second did I ever think you were part of this. I never thought that even for a second," Lisa answered while wrapping Clay in a hug. Even as she said those words to Clay, she shuddered as a chill ran down her spine. She found herself thinking back to just minutes ago. Minutes ago, as she was handcuffing the suspects while Clay provided cover from behind her, the thought had occurred to her, "What if Clay is in on this?" She even imagined a bullet from Clay's rifle hitting her in the back. But the momentary thought was just that, a thought and a ridiculous one at that. Clay, she then realized, was not just a partner; he was like a father to her.

"I guess we better call Sean," Lisa told Clay.

Clay looked at his watch and answered, "Fuck Sean. He's probably still sleeping."

Just then, Clay noticed the first emergency vehicle coming down the short hill to their location, followed by a whole string of first responders. Clay knew only four-wheel-drive vehicles could make it all the way into their location.

"Looks like the cavalry is here. I'll just ask State Patrol radio to notify Sean," Lisa said.

Within minutes, four deputies had arrived, one with a trooper sitting on the passenger side of his SUV.

One of the responders yelled out, "Is the scene clear?"

242

"All clear and weapons secured," Lisa answered back. "Two suspects. One in cuffs and one down on the ground with gunshot wounds to the chest."

"Are both of you okay?" asked Okanogan County Sheriff's Office Sgt. Jake Miller, the first responder on the scene.

"We are good. The only injuries are the gunshot wounds on him," Lisa said as she pointed at Moe.

"The ambulance couldn't make it up this road, so we will need to transport the suspect back to the main road, and the best vehicle for that would be your truck," Sgt. Jake Miller said as he scoped out the entire scene. "Why don't you two stay here, and I will drive the injured guy back down and will transfer your prisoner to my vehicle."

"Please thoroughly search them before you take them. I already searched them, but we were a bit hurried," Lisa suggested.

"Will do. Thanks for the heads up," the Sarge responded.

Three men helped load Moe in the bed of Lisa's truck and slowly worked their way over the hill and down the other side.

"What happened here?" asked one of the deputies.

"Look, we will be glad to answer everyone's questions once we both get a chance to call our spouses," Clay told the deputy.

The deputy looked at Lisa and answered, "Well, your spouse is on her way, and judging by her response on the radio, she is probably moving at the speed of light to get here. I fully understand. Please make the calls you need to make. Our talk can wait."

243

"We got the bad guys, but Lisa had to shoot one of them," Clay told Karen through tears.

"Oh my god, are you both okay?" Karen answered on the edge of panic.

"Not a scratch on either one of us, but Lisa saved my life. I froze, and she didn't. I would be dead if it weren't for her," Clay muttered softly.

"God bless her. Tell her I said thank you. You have the best partner on earth."

"I had the best partner on earth. I'm done. My career is over," Clay cried to Karen.

"Why would you say that? It sounds like everything worked out as well as it could under the circumstances," Karen said.

"Because it was Moe. Moe was the bad guy. Moe is the one who tried to kill us. Moe is the person Lisa shot. I'm done, Karen. Nobody will believe that I had nothing to do with my best friend running a poaching and smuggling operation without me knowing about it. I just hope I get to keep my retirement."

"Oh my god! Is Moe alive?"

"Unfortunately, he is," Clay answered.

"Clay, you don't really mean that. Can I come to wherever you are?" Karen asked.

244

"Sorry, but that can't happen. I will be home in a few hours. I'm sorry for everything. I screwed everything up. It's all on me," Clay answered. "Hey, I better get going. I will call when I get a chance."

"What do I say to Garma? Does she even know?" Karen asked.

"Oh crap, I forgot about her and the girls. Until the county talks to everyone, I think you should just keep it all to yourself."

"It will be okay, you will see. It will all work out. You're a good man, and everyone knows it. I love you," Karen said as they ended the call.

Before Sgt. Miller returned, Clay pulled Lisa away from the only deputy left behind with them and asked, "You knew, didn't you? You didn't hesitate even a second. You weren't surprised. You already knew it was Moe, didn't you?"

"I didn't know for sure, but I thought it was possible," Lisa said. "He just has too much money, and there were some other things that just made me wonder."

"So, you figure out that it's Moe, but you don't even tell me. You don't trust me now if you ever did. You thought I was in on all of this shit, huh?" Clay said.

"No, no, no. I didn't share it with you because I wasn't sure, and I had no idea Moe would be here. I just thought it would be a big distraction for you while we were following Matt. I was going to talk to you about it as soon as we were done with whatever this was. I swear," Lisa explained.

245

Clay spun around on his heels and walked away from Lisa.

About ten minutes after their phone calls, Sgt. Miller returned, driving his patrol vehicle with Matt Davis in the back, followed by the unmarked truck driven by one of the deputies.

"All right. Mr. Ohmar is on the way to Omak General, and Mr. Davis is sitting comfortably in my backseat. Everyone is safe, and the sun is finally up. So, what was this all about anyway?" asked Sgt. Miller.

"I guess I have no idea," Clay said in disgust. "Apparently, I have had my head so far up my ass, I haven't had a clue about what's going on all around me."

"Let's just start with tonight. What brought you here, and how did this end up the way it did?" Sgt. Miller asked.

"It's a long story, but we had reason to believe that Matt Davis was involved in a commercial poaching, smuggling, and drug operation, but we didn't know much else. Tonight, we followed him here in an effort to figure out what he was up to, which took us to this," Lisa explained.

"As we were walking in to get a better look, we heard a drone coming closer. The drone landed. The suspects picked it up, flipped it over, and opened that box sitting on Matt's tailgate. They then dumped the contents out, just as you see them. We haven't touched any of that. Anyway, as we approached them, we identified ourselves and commanded them to put their hands up and kneel down. Matt followed our instructions, while the other subject did not. We didn't

246

know it was Moe at that time. Moe pulled a gun out of his waistband, turned, and pointed it directly at us. That's when I fired," Lisa explained

"But you never fired? Why not?" Sgt. Miller asked Clay.

"Because I'm an idiot, and I froze. When I saw it was Moe, I just froze and didn't do a thing. If it wasn't for Lisa, we wouldn't be alive right now," Clay said in shame. "Hell, even when the taxidermist yelled "gun" to warn us, I still did nothing."

"The other suspect warned you about Moe having a gun in his hands?" Miller asked.

"Yeah, he did. I totally forgot about that until just now. That was pretty weird," Lisa said.

"So, what's in the packages?" the Sergeant asked.

"We have no idea. We never got a chance to look," Lisa answered.

"Let's go take a look at what was so important to these guys," the Sergeant said as he walked to Matt's truck.

On the tailgate were five separate bundles wrapped in cellophane and tape. Further up toward the cab, in the pickup's bed, were four Ziplock bags full of what Clay identified as dried bear gallbladders.

Sergeant Miller picked up one bundle and bounced it around in his hand. "It weighs around a kilo, so I'm going to go out on a limb here and guess it's dope," Miller announced as he walked over to his truck to grab some Nik presumptive drug tests.

247

"Yep, that was the incoming delivery, and the bear gallbladder were the outgoing delivery. Bear gallbladder for dope—right in front of me," Clay remarked.

Back at Matt's truck, Miller donned latex gloves before carefully pushing a knife into one of the packages. He pulled the knife out, leaving a small sample on the tip.

"Looks like crystal," Miller announced as he dropped the sample into the open Nik test, cracked the glass vial in the test bag, then shook it vigorously before holding it up to the light. "Yep, it's meth. It looks like you just seized 5 kilos of meth. Good work, guys."

"You want us to handle the evidence?" Miller asked.

"We would appreciate that, Jake. Thanks. I think we will have our hands plenty full for the next few days," Clay answered as he handed Sgt. Miller the pistol he had taken from Moe.

At that very moment, Emily came running down the hill to Lisa. After Emily had spoken privately to Lisa, they both walked over to Clay.

"Clay, I told Lisa I would suggest neither of you say any more until you have spoken to your guild lawyers. I trust all of these guys with my life, but I would never give them a statement without my legal representative present," Emily explained.

"You're right, especially for me. Lisa was flawless. I'm the one who screwed up. I'm the one who's going to need a lawyer. Thanks," Clay said as he walked away to be alone.

248

As if Clay needed more stress, the next vehicle down the hill was driven by Sgt. Dresken.

"You guys need to fill me in on just what the hell happened here this morning. Jesus Christ, I said catch 'em, not kill 'em," Sean said as he approached Clay and Lisa.

In an instant, before Lisa could say a word, Clay exploded, "No, really Sean, we are both okay, but thanks for asking, asshole. You wanna know what's going on, Sean boy? It's simple. I quit," Clay said between gritted teeth, "and you can shove this up your ass." Clay then tore the badge from his shirt, thrusting it into Sean's chest with enough force to rock him back on his heels.

"Yeah, well, maybe that's best for everyone, old man," Sean answered.

Clay just stared at Sean before saying, "Get the hell out of my way before I kick the living shit out of you."

As Clay began walking up the hill, he realized he didn't have a vehicle, and Lisa was his ride home.

"Lisa, give me a ride home," Clay asked.

"She's not going anywhere, especially with your duty weapons. I need you two to surrender your weapons. You know the policy," Sean said.

For the first time since they had started walking that night, Clay put down his AR-15. As he walked by Sean's truck, he dropped the AR on his front seat, followed by his entire duty belt with the pistol, his ballistic vest, and uniform shirt, leaving Clay walking away in a white T-shirt and uniform pants.

"I'll take you back," Sgt. Miller told Clay. "I need to get your taxidermist buddy to the jail anyway. Once we get him booked, I will take you home. Let's hit it."

"Thanks," Clay said as he climbed into the front passenger seat of the Sergeant's vehicle.

As the three men started the hour-plus drive to Omak, Sgt. Miller turned to Matt and asked, "So, why did you warn the officers that your buddy had a gun? You thought it was your opportunity to take over the business or something?"

"I'm pretty sure you won't believe me, so I will hold off on that answer for a while," Matt said.

"Look, asshole, I'm not in the mood for games. Just answer the fucking question," Clay demanded.

"Okay. You want the answer. I warned you because I didn't want your partner to get shot, and I wanted to see how you were going to react? Well, I saw how you reacted. You lowered your rifle and just let it play out. You were just going to stand by and let your best buddy on earth kill your partner, but it didn't work out that way, did it?" Matt answered. "What was supposed to be your next move? Were you going to kill me too?"

At that moment, Clay wished he hadn't turned his pistol over to Boy Wonder. As he seethed, Clay visualized putting a bullet right in the middle of Matt's head. He was so furious, he could have killed Matt with his bare hands and very much wanted to at that moment.

Sgt. Miller advised both men to tone it down and knock it off, "Come on, you guys, we have a long drive. You both just need to zip it."

"Sergeant Miller, just for my safety, I want to give you my full name. I am U.S. Fish and Wildlife Service Special Agent, Matthew R. Daniels. I am actively undercover at this time, but I will provide you with my supervisor's contact information for confirmation once we get to your jail. Just keep this crooked, psycho piece of shit away from me, or there will be hell to pay for all of you."

CHAPTER 36

"I think you better just stay in the car while I book him. You two don't play well together," Sgt. Miller said as they were pulling up to the jail's sally port.

Miller opened the right-rear door of his patrol vehicle and guided their prisoner out and onto his feet, but before the backdoor closed, Matt leaned in and addressed Clay, "Today, you temporarily put me in jail, but I promise you that soon I will be booking your ass into jail, but it will be for a very long time. I hate crooked cops."

Sgt. Miller walked the prisoner in the man-door of the sally port, where they were met by three very large and unfriendly-looking corrections officers. The jailers uncuffed and searched Matt thoroughly before one officer waved his arm to the controller, who remotely opened the door to the booking desk.

Once at the booking desk, Matt turned and asked Sgt. Miller, "Are you ready for some names and phone numbers, so we can clear this up without wasting more of anyone's time?"

"Sure, knock yourself out," Jake told Matt.

"Okay. The first is my SAC (Special Agent in Charge) Rick Magill, in California, at 916-555-9330. Next is AUSA (Assistant United States Attorney) Brock Shay, out of Spokane, 509-555-1693. When you talk to either one of them, they will ask you for the name of the operation and the extract phrase. It's Operation Northern Lights, and the extract phrase is; Golden Bear. Please give them a call right away, so I can get to work instead of spending quality time with the prisoners here," Matt said sarcastically.

"Continue the booking process while I make a couple of calls," Sgt. Miller told the jail staff at the intake counter as he turned to walk away.

"Wait a second," Sgt. Miller said before walking back to Matt and taking a full-face picture of him with his cell phone.

Jake Miller then took his cell phone into one of the interview rooms for some privacy. Suspicious of the information Matt had provided to him, Jake looked up the office number for the AUSA in Spokane for himself, and then he called. After working his way through the gauntlet, he was finally put through to AUSA Brock Shay.

"Mr. Shay, my name is Sgt. Jake Miller, and I'm with the Okanogan County Sheriff's Office. I don't even know how to start here. Early this morning, we had an officer-involved shooting. One of our fish and wildlife officers shot a suspect and took a second subject into custody. The second subject is known to us as Matthew B. Davis. On our way to the jail, Mr. Davis informed me his real name was actually Matthew R. Daniels and that he is an undercover agent with the U.S Fish and Wildlife Service. Mr. Davis, Daniels, or whoever he is, has not been injured, nor has anyone other than the other suspect who, as we speak, is in the emergency room."

"I see," Shay said before a long pause. "Did Mr. Daniels happen to mention an operation name?"

253

"Operation Northern Lights with an extract phrase of golden bear. I also took a photo of him, and I can text or email it if you give me a number or email address," said Miller in response.

"Please, text the photo to my cell phone at (509) 555-1693, and I will call you right back after I get it," Shay instructed Sgt. Miller.

"That number matches the phone number Matt told me to call."

"Then I have to ask, why did you call my office line instead of my cell?" asked Shay.

"Because he's the one who gave me the number, I would have had no idea who I would really be talking to on that phone."

"Smart and cautious. I like it," replied Shay. "Once I get that pic, I will make some calls and get right back to you."

"It's on the way," Jake Miller said as he sent the photo, "and by the way, your Mr. Daniels has a very big mouth, which I think might get him in some trouble, so if I were you, I would remind him of his right to remain silent."

Next came the call to the SAC. Despite Sgt. Miller's best efforts, he could not find any reference to SAC Rick Magill on the internet, but he did confirm that area code 916 was for Sacramento, CA. He decided just to call the California office for USFWS law enforcement for the Pacific Southwest Region.

Sgt. Miller explained to the receptionist that it was an emergency and he needed to speak to SAC Magill right away. Without confirming or denying she had ever even heard of SAC Rick Magill, the

254

receptionist answered in a polite and professional manner, "I'm sorry, but may I take your name and have someone call you right back?"

Less than ten minutes after placing the call to California, Sgt. Miller's phone indicated the incoming call was from (916) 555-9330, the same number Matt had provided for his boss.

"Sergeant Miller, my name is Rick Magill, and I understand you have some sort of emergency you wanted to speak to me about?" asked Magill.

Miller then found himself in the same conversation he just had with the AUSA from Spokane. But this time, Mr. Magill's voice had some urgency in it.

"What's it takes to drive to Omak from Spokane—three hours or so?" Magill asked.

"Yeah, that's about right in good weather."

"Sgt. Miller, I will give your sheriff a call, right after we are done, to ask the same of him as I am now going to ask of you. First, you can continue booking Mr. Davis/Daniels on whatever charges you want if you feel it's still necessary, but please do not put him in general population—for obvious reasons. Secondly, please ensure this information is kept confidential. Tell nobody about any of this. Next, there will be at least two federal agents in your sheriff's office within four hours, and I am sure RAC (Resident Agent in Charge) Ross Crenshaw will join them as soon as possible. I would ask that both you and your sheriff be present," Magill explained. "Will that work for you?"

"No problem at all, except I don't schedule the Sheriff's time," answered Sgt. Miller.

"Understood. Sergeant Miller, I do have one more request. Would it be possible for me to speak to your prisoner for a few seconds?"

"I guess under the circumstances that would be okay, but I will need to be in the room to monitor," Miller answered.

Sgt. Miller stepped out of the interview room and waved to get the attention of one of the officers at the intake counter. "Hey, send Mr. Daniels over here, would ya?"

Daniels, who was now cuffed in front, joined Miller in the interview room. "Someone wants to talk to you," he said.

As Daniels received the phone from Miller, he asked, "Do you mind Deputy Barney? How about a little privacy?"

"You have two minutes. I wouldn't waste them talking to me if I were you," Miller responded as he moved even closer to him.

For the next couple of minutes, Sgt. Miller heard the undercover fed explain how poorly he had been treated, how he wanted out by nightfall, and how corrupt Clay was.

At the two-minute mark, Miller reached over and snatched the phone out of Daniels's hand, hung it up, and announced, "Time's up."

As Sgt. Miller walked through the first sliding door to the outside, he turned and told Daniels, "I hope you enjoy your stay with us, officer. The showers can be especially fun. Come on back again."

"You can count on it, Barney," was the only response.

As Jake walked out of the jail, he noticed Clay sitting on a short retainer wall—just staring ahead.

"Come on, buddy, let's get you home," Sgt. Miller said.

"So, is he really a fed?" Clay asked as both men got back into Sgt. Miller's patrol vehicle.

"It kinda looks that way, yeah."

"What was he doing here?" Clay asked.

"Other than being a total asshole, I'm not sure, but it looks to me like he is here to investigate you. He seems to have a hard-on for you," said Miller.

"Me. He's investigating me for what?"

"I don't know that either, my friend, but I think you better get a good lawyer. The only thing I was told was that all of this has to stay confidential," Miller answered.

After going no more than a mile, Clay's cell phone began vibrating. Clay looked at the screen and pushed the decline button, putting the phone back in his pocket.

"Who was that?"

"Lisa. It's about the tenth call from her in the last half-hour," Clay responded.

Jake thought about asking why Clay was declining his partner's calls, but he decided to stay out of it, thinking the less he knew, the better.

As the Sergeant pulled in front of Clay's home, he put his hand out to Clay to shake and said, "Anytime, 24-hours a day, any day, you need anything, call me. If you want someone to talk to, call me. I'm telling you, all the guys in our department would walk through fire to help you, so don't forget your extended family. You are our brother, and we are all here for you, and I mean it. The same goes for Lisa."

"Thanks, man. I do appreciate it, but right now, I don't even know what's going on. This morning we were hunting a bad guy, and now I am the bad guy," Clay said.

"Thanks again," Clay said as he walked to the front door of his home.

CHAPTER 37

"He thinks I betrayed him," Lisa told Emily once they were finally alone, "and I guess I did."

"Lisa, you didn't betray him in any way. You were just doing your job, and you faced horrible choices. He will come around to understanding it."

"Clay knows I had reason to believe it was Moe, and I didn't tell him. He thinks I don't trust him and that I think he was in on all of this mess from the start," Lisa answered.

"What did make you believe it might be Moe?" Emily asked.

"In the afternoon before the shooting, I got on the FlashFone website and saw there was a place to enter your zip code to see where the closest FlashFone vendor was located. When I put in the zip code for Oroville, the only business that came up was Moe-Mart. The thing is, I have been in Moe-Mart a hundred times, and he doesn't sell FlashFones, or at least he doesn't display them. I just didn't know how to even talk to Clay about Moe possibly being involved, and just because Moe does or did sell FlashFones, doesn't mean those phones came from him. We won't know that until we get the return on our warrant."

"Well, is there a chance, even a slight one, that Clay was involved?"

"Are you kidding? Absolutely not! Not possible. Clay is the most honorable man I have ever met. There is no way he did this. It was all Moe and that taxidermist," Lisa answered angrily. "I can't believe you would say that!"

"Hey, calm down. I'm on your side. I was just asking—not suggesting anything," Emily explained.

"I know. It's just that this is such a mess right now. Moe is probably dead by now, and my partner just quit the department and won't even talk to me anymore. We started with a poaching case and ended up with me shooting Clay's best friend. Oh god, this is all screwed up," Lisa said with tears pouring down her face.

"What time is your meeting with your guild rep on Monday?" Emily asked.

"He said he would be at our house by eleven a.m. Why?" Lisa asked.

"Because I want to be here for it," Emily said. "I'll bet Chelan County will handle the shooting investigation, and I want to make sure you are represented at all the steps through this process."

"You think the guild will still represent Clay, even though he quit?"

Emily answered, "I don't know, but right now, we have to focus on you."

"And just leave Clay swinging in the wind?"

"That's not what I mean, and you know it," Emily said.

CHAPTER 38

Sheriff Kevin Bryant had asked for the county prosecutor to
attend the meeting, on a Saturday morning, with the two federal agents,
RAC (Resident Agent in Charge), Ross Crenshaw, and the AUSA,
making for a crowded office. As the elected county prosecutor
continued reading the documents, which the federal prosecutor had just
handed him, RAC Crenshaw spoke, "As you can see, the operation has
stayed within the laws and policies of the federal government all
through the investigation. Our undercover agent conducted himself
professionally and properly throughout his involvement in the
operation and in no way had any idea Mr. Ohmar was armed. In fact,
our agent saved the female wildlife officer's life by warning her when
he observed Mr. Ohmar's pistol, apparently before she did.

The RAC went on, "While the shooting was regrettable, our agent
had absolutely no role in the violence other than to try to protect the
wildlife officer."

It was then Tony's turn, "I'm not sure why you refer to only a
singular "wildlife officer" and not both officers. You do know there
were two state officers present, not just the female officer?"

RAC Crenshaw answered, "I did not do so to offend anyone in
any manner, but it is our understanding that Officer Newberry may not
be the innocent victim he portrays himself to be and thus may not have
been in danger himself."

Sheriff Bryant addressed the RAC, "That is probably the most
asinine thing I have ever heard come out of someone's mouth. In our

261

county, everybody is innocent until proven guilty, even our cops. I just hope you remember that before you ruin a good man's career."

"Well, I guess that will depend on if Mr. Newberry is in fact a good man, won't it?" answered Crenshaw.

"Would you be willing to enlighten us on just what led you to place an undercover federal agent into a taxidermy shop in Oroville?" Tony asked.

"I'm sorry, but at this time, that information is still confidential."

"So, Sheriff, what exactly do we need to do to get our guy out of your jail?" one of the other federal agents asked.

Sheriff Bryant looked at the county prosecutor, who gave him a head nod before saying, "I will make the call right away, and you can pick him up anytime you want."

"Great, and thanks," one of the federal agents said as the group of feds stood to leave.

"Not so fast," Sheriff Bryant said. "I want to make a couple of things perfectly clear. None of my people answer to you. If you want something from us, you will go through me first. If you want one of our people to help you in your investigation, I will gladly assign one of our detectives to assist, but it will be at my direction. Last, I have known Clay Newberry for my entire career, and I find your accusations to be ridiculous and slanderous. I suggest you and your undercover guy keep your opinions to yourself until you prove them to be facts. Are we clear?"

"Perfectly," RAC Crenshaw said as he walked out.

Once outside, the RAC addressed the other special agents, "I should have the warrants signed and in your hands by five this afternoon. Make sure and notify the Sheriff that you are serving the warrants—right after you begin searching. And keep Daniels in the shadows until we are done here. He has the locals pissed off enough already. And, somebody find out if Ohmar is going to make it or not. Keep me posted."

CHAPTER 39

It was a warm, sunny, and quiet Sunday morning as Lisa, who hadn't slept more than three hours the previous night, sat staring out into their backyard. She played the shooting over and over in her head, wondering what would have happened if she had done this rather than that. It wasn't the shooting that kept her awake at night; she knew she had no choice there. It was Clay.

Other than Emily, she had never trusted anyone as much as she trusted Clay. Now she knew Clay was mad, hurt, confused, and scared. For the first time in days, Lisa smiled as she realized she had never seen Clay even concerned, let alone scared. Everything was screwed up. Sean wanted Clay fired. The feds wanted him in jail, and she had killed his best friend.

Emily had received a phone call late the night before, informing her that Moe had died due to his injuries. She thought about not telling Lisa since she already had enough stress but decided she had to know. Emily hated doing it, but she had relayed that information to Lisa, knowing it would add to her inability to get any sleep.

Of course, all involved parties were told they could not discuss the incident with each other, but that did not mean they couldn't talk about anything else either.

When Emily awoke, Lisa was already up. Emily headed to the kitchen, where she saw Lisa sitting on the back deck, staring off into space.

Emily knew Lisa had a roster of all of the addresses and phone numbers of both the officers and their spouses, which was updated by the department each year. Emily pulled the roster from their home office and looked up Karen Newberry's cell number.

Emily thought about it for a while and then started the text, "Karen, this is Emily. I can only imagine what you and Clay are going through right now, and it makes my heartache. As you can imagine, this is consuming Lisa right now—with the biggest issue being her friendship with Clay. I was wondering if you think it's about time we get these two together and give them some time alone. If it's too soon, I understand. Take care."

Within two minutes, Emily received her response, "Oh my god, you are so right. Please, please, please come up to our house at any time. We will be here with the blinds drawn as we hide from the world. Clay needs to talk to someone, and I don't know how to help him. I can't think of a better idea. Bless you."

On her way out to the porch, she poured a cup of coffee. "Morning. How long have you been up?"

"Off and on all night. I just can't turn it off."

"Do you need a refill before we get ready for the day?" Emily asked.

"I'm good. Thanks."

"All right, here's what we are going to do today. We are both going to take our time getting ready, and then we are driving up to visit Clay and Karen."

265

"Clay doesn't want to see me. He won't even return my calls."

"He may not want to see anyone, but he needs to see you. I just heard from Karen, and she said Clay's in a really bad place, and she doesn't know what to do to help him."

"I guess he would normally talk to his best friend, but I killed him."

"Well, that's done, and nothing will change that, but now Clay needs to be saved by his other best friend. So, let's get going."

Forty-five minutes later, they were knocking on the Newberry's front door. Almost immediately, Karen opened the front door and invited them in.

Karen got everyone's attention and then announced, "Okay, you two, here's what's going to happen. Emily and I are heading to the Sportsman's for breakfast. You two need to talk, so I expect you both to do just that. We will be back in an hour or so. Any questions? Okay, great. See you in an hour."

Forty-five minutes later, Emily looked up to see Clay and Lisa walking into the cafe together. Then something happened that none of the four of them ever would have predicted. First one, then another, then every customer and employee in the café gave Clay and Lisa a standing ovation before each of them came up to personally offer their support. It was only the second time that Karen had ever seen Clay cry. The first time was the day before.

As Clay and Lisa sat at the table, Clay simply said, "We're good. Thanks to you two."

266

CHAPTER 40

It was 8:20 on Monday morning when two large SUVs pulled in front of the Newberry's home. Clay answered the knock on his door, only to find a half-dozen federal agents lined up on his driveway. The lead agent, who identified himself as Resident Agent in Charge Ross Crenshaw, handed Clay a copy of the warrant to search his home.

Crenshaw was polite and professional, even apologizing for the inconvenience, but obviously was not about to change his mind regarding the search of Clay and Karen's home.

Clay and Karen were given the option of staying in the home, but only if they remained seated and out of the way or leaving, but were told if they left, they would not be allowed back in until the search was completed. They opted to stay put on their large sofa.

As five agents entered their home and began searching, Clay could hear Agent Crenshaw on his phone, notifying someone of the search in progress. Clay could tell the conversation wasn't going very well for Crenshaw.

As the federal agents combed through his home, Clay and Karen read the warrant. The warrant allowed for the search of the Newberry's home, grounds, vehicles, and the person of Clay Newberry. Since Clay had not yet been searched or even patted down, they wondered when that piece of the search would come into play.

Well, at least they aren't searching Karen's person, Clay thought.

The warrant allowed the agents to search for narcotics, cash, gallbladder and/or other bear parts, flight controllers and/or drones or parts thereof, computers, external memory devices, records or documents, photos, videos, and cellular phones.

As Karen began to cry, Clay's fury began to rise.

"How long will this bullshit take?" Clay asked one of the younger agents in his home.

"We will be done when we are done. So, if you don't like it, then leave," said the young agent.

Clay thought about how much had changed in less than a week. He went from a law enforcement officer involved in the largest wildlife trafficking case in the state's history to an unemployed criminal suspect. He never thought there would be a time when he would consider any law enforcement officers to be his enemies, but that time had come.

Karen and Clay sat together, watching as strange men went through every nook and cranny of their modest home. They discussed whether they would be better off leaving or staying and decided to continue to stay and monitor the search, even though they were not allowed to move from the couch.

At 9:15, Clay heard some loud arguing in front of his house and opened the curtains behind the couch to see what the raucous was all about. What Clay saw was Deputy Emily Bennington in full uniform, absolutely reaming Agent Crenshaw a new one. Every time Crenshaw opened his mouth to speak, Emily cut him off and yelled at the agent even louder. As Clay watched, he saw Sheriff Kevin Bryant walk right past Agent Crenshaw and in through Clay's open front door.

"How are you two holding up?" Sheriff Bryant asked.

"Never better," Clay answered. "I assume this is all because I disrespected their undercover guy or something. What I can't understand is how they convinced a judge to sign this bullshit warrant."

"Clay, just keep calm, let them do their thing, and when they are done here, I'm going to put a stop to this, and I mean quick," the Sheriff said. "Just hang in there and let the men in black complete their search."

As the Sheriff spoke, Clay noticed him looking out the window behind their heads, so Clay turned to see what was so interesting. He then noticed Trooper Greer, Prosecutor Tony Breckler, and no less than three deputies standing in his driveway with an additional dozen or so of his neighbors out on the road. The neighbors were wondering what was going on while the officers were grumbling about this federal over-reach.

"Where in the hell is SAC Magill?" Breckler asked RAC Crenshaw.

"He's at one of the other search locations."

"What other locations?"

"We are also currently searching Moe Ohmar's business and home," answered Crenshaw.

269

"Would you please get him on the phone for me?" Breckler asked the agent.

"Agent Magill, this is Tony Breckler, the prosecutor for this county. I was wondering if I could persuade you and AUSA Shay to meet with the Sheriff and myself when your searches are completed? A huge shitstorm is brewing here, and I think we are the four people who have the best opportunity to calm things down."

"Well, both of us will be here at least another day or two, so how about we meet at your office, say around four p.m. this afternoon?"

"We will see you then. Thanks for agreeing to meet with us," Breckler said as the call ended.

Noting the disapproval on Emily's face, Breckler said to her, "Just remember, you can catch more flies with sugar than with vinegar."

"These guys aren't flies. They're maggots," Emily replied.

"I'm surprised Lisa isn't here," the Sheriff commented.

"Today is her day to meet the guild representative and give her statement to the department, regarding the shooting. I was not allowed to attend that meeting to support my wife, so I came here to support our friend."

"Thanks. They need all of our support, now more than ever," the Sheriff added.

CHAPTER 41

With the four men sitting around a conference table in the prosecutor's office, SAC Rick Magill opened the conversation.

"May before last, TSA caught a guy at Sea-Tac airport with forty-something dried bear gallbladders taped to his body under his clothing. The subject was Burmese and from Myanmar. On his visa application, the subject had declared that the purpose of his trip was to visit a family member in Oroville, WA. The TSA agent called in the U.S. Fish and Wildlife uniformed inspector, who, in total error, seized the gallbladder, issued the subject a simple citation, and allowed him to board his flight home. That mistake is totally on that one uniformed officer, but we can't exactly require the guy to come back to face felony charges when he already paid his citation for his crimes.

"A check of immigration records showed only one Burmese family living in Oroville, and I guess we all know who they are. We did some checking on Mr. Ohmar and learned he was the former commander of the Myanmar National Police, so we decided that just showing up at his door and asking for consent to search would be futile. Another thing we learned when we started looking at Moe Ohmar was the reason he left Myanmar. He was about two days away from being arrested for his role in leading a criminal organization involved in elephant poaching, ivory trafficking, and narcotics manufacturing. INS was already looking into revoking his resident alien status due to his providing false information on his immigration application.

"Added to all that, we had a CI (Confidential Informant) who is an enrolled tribal member and told us Moe was involved in a drugs for gall scheme. So that's what brought us here.

"So then, our UC started getting close to the target, but your Warden Clay got all jealous and tried like hell to pin something on Daniels, or as you know him, Matt Davis. Daniels got closer to Moe until finally, Moe asked him to use his taxidermy contacts to get him all the gallbladder he could find. Moe even gave the UC a free cell phone. Then he had him running all over hell, picking up gall from his other runners. The whole time, Moe was telling Daniels that Clay was telling Moe that the taxidermist is bad news and can't be trusted. Hell, Warden Clay practically lives with Moe, they are so tight.

"Daniels got deeper and deeper, meeting more of Moe's inner circle. Then one day, Moe handed Daniels a new cell phone. Moe told Daniels they all had to switch phones because the game wardens were getting a warrant for the phone records of their burners. Daniels asked what made him think that, and Moe just told him his buddy Clay had warned him.

"You know Warden Clay can claim ignorance all he wants, but Jesus, just Google Myanmar someday. It's the second-largest producer of heroin and is on the way to becoming the largest producer of meth. On top of it all, Myanmar is famous for smuggling ivory out and bear gallbladder in. It's all over the internet. When we looked up Moe's name, we found the English translation of the Burmese name Moe is rain, like in Rainman. A third-grader would have figured this out," the SAC finished.

272

Tony Breckler leaned in and said, "Okay, now it's my turn. Need I remind you it was Clay who started this whole investigation. It was Clay who complained to his bosses, over and over, until he got proper surveillance equipment. Lisa will confirm that it was Clay who insisted on conducting the surveillance, which led to the apprehension of your agent as well as Moe Ohmar. Without Clay, your agent would have had all the glory to himself and would not have to share credit for bringing down this international smuggler. Now he has to share the credit with a lowly state warden. I think that proves who the jealous one was, and that same agent had already decided to pin some of this shitshow on Clay for revenge. So instead of persecuting Clay, you should be apologizing to him. You all have tarnished the outstanding record of an honorable, hard-working law enforcement officer.

"I am proud to say Clay is my friend. I trusted him before this, and I still trust him today. The only thing Clay is guilty of is believing in his friends a bit too much.

"Look, gentlemen, we all can have a win here. Your guy did great work, and together we will bring down some really bad guys and will save lives—both humans and wildlife. There is no reason we can't all come out of this smelling like roses. I understand the only item of potential evidentiary value you removed from Clay's home was his personal laptop computer. Have that cloned and analyzed, and when you find nothing, because there never was anything there, you will return his property. When you return that property, you will tell him thank you, and you will apologize for the inconvenience. You can explain how you were only doing your jobs, and Clay will say he understands, and then we all go our separate ways. We come out

273

looking like the poster children for the interagency cooperation campaign. Sound like something you can live with?" Breckler asked as he concluded.

It was AUSA Shay's turn to speak. "For as long as I can remember, there has been a deep-seated hostility toward the federal government in this county, and it's time that changes. We are all on the same team and are all better than this. Together we need to show the community that we trust each other. That will not happen by having stand-offs between your deputies and federal agents like we experienced at Officer Newberry's home this morning.

"If Newberry's computer comes back clean, you have a deal. We need to all focus on Moe Ohmar and his criminal organization, rather than on each other," AUSA Shay added.

AUSA Shay then directed his attention to SAC Magill. "Rick, I want you to have Officer Newberry's computer processed as soon as humanly possible. I do not want this hanging over Newberry's head for months. Get this done ASAP."

"We will get on it immediately and should have the findings in three days or less," SAC Magill answered.

"Great. Now, Agent Magill, I think we owe these gentlemen a dinner," said the Assistant U.S. Attorney.

It was very apparent to everyone around the conference table that SAC Magill was not happy with the agreement Shay had made with the locals but was smart enough to keep his mouth shut.

By the time the four men finally sat down to eat a meal together, it was almost six p.m. By then, SAC Magill seemed to have calmed down substantially and was much more congenial. At the Sheriff's insistence, the men had decided to eat the "best Mexican food they had ever tried."

Sheriff Bryant was about halfway through his meal at Miguel's when his cell phone rang. Sheriff Bryant noticed the call was from his dispatch center, so he excused himself to take the call outside. Five minutes later, Sheriff Bryant handed AUSA Shay a note with a phone number.

"Garma Ohmar would like to speak to you directly and as soon as possible. She said she has some valuable information but will only deal with you," Bryant said.

"I will return her call as soon as we are done here. Thanks for passing on the message, Sheriff."

At about 6:45 AUSA, Shay returned the call to Moe's wife.

"Mrs. Ohmar, this is Assistant U.S. Attorney Brock Shay, and I understand you want to speak to me."

"Well, I wanted to talk to the head guy for the federal police, but Sheriff Bryant said it would be better if I spoke with you instead."

Her comment made Shay grin. "What can I do for you?"

"Moe was a great father and a good husband, but he also had a dark side that few knew about. The real reason we left our home in Myanmar was because of Moe's illegal actions. I love Moe, but he

275

was doing very bad things at home, which eventually led to our family being banished from our homeland. We left everything behind. When we arrived in Canada, Moe promised me that he would never get back to that life again and would do things within the law for our family," Garma said through tears. "But, once again, Moe lied to me. He went right back to what got us kicked out of Myanmar. He shamed our family once again and put our lives in danger.

"The girls and I cannot go back to Myanmar. To do so would mean we would all be executed. We want to stay right here, and I want my girls to be raised as honest, hard-working American children with all the opportunities available here.

"I know little of what Moe's criminal activities were here, but I certainly know who he would work with in Canada and Myanmar, and that should be of help in your investigation. Do you think that if I tell you everything I know, we could stay?"

"I can't make any promises, but if you can help facilitate our investigation, it would certainly be considered in your immigration status," Shay said. "Can we meet tomorrow to talk?"

Shay and Garma agreed to meet at Ohmar's home in the morning.

CHAPTER 42

On Thursday, Agents Crenshaw and Magill found themselves standing at the front door of Clay's home with his personal laptop in hand.

As SAC Rick Magill handed the laptop to Clay, he said, "Officer Newberry, it is with our sincere apology that we would like to return this. I know this has put you through hell, and there is simply no way to make that up to you. I do want you to know that we are working in conjunction with the Sheriff's office and your agency to draft a joint statement regarding the investigation. You, and your partner, will be recognized for your courageous performance and tenacity. Again, thanks for your great work, and we are very sorry about the misunderstanding."

"Misunderstanding huh? Is that what that was? Get the hell off my property before I really do commit a crime," Clay said as he slammed the door shut.

Three hours after the feds left his house, Clay received a text from Lisa. "Clay, can you please meet me at the detachment office tomorrow morning around eight. We need to talk about what I still have to do to finish up this case. I can't complete this without your help."

"I will be there. I will need you to give me a ride home because I'm leaving my patrol vehicle there for someone to take back to Olympia. See you in the morning."

Clay suspected there was more to the office invitation than what Lisa had told him but figured he would find out tomorrow. Maybe he was going to be arrested this time.

At 7:40 on Friday morning, Clay parked directly in front of the detachment office, adjacent to Lisa's truck, which did not allow him to see the rear parking area.

Before walking into the office, Clay scooped up a box of miscellaneous department-issued items, which he carried in with him. When Clay stepped in the room, he was genuinely surprised to see both WDFW Chief Jim Gassett and SIU Captain Aaron Hamlin.

"What's this, some kind of intervention or something?" Clay asked.

"Yeah, I guess you might say that. We just want to make sure we do our best to avoid losing one of our best officers," replied the chief.

"I appreciate that, but I've talked it over with my wife and have decided it's time for me to go."

"We aren't talking about you dipshit," Aaron said with a wide grin. "It's Lisa we are worried about losing."

"It seems your partner here doesn't think you have been treated properly and said that if you go, she will accept the Sheriff's job offer here," added Chief Gassett. "While I'm not a fan of being blackmailed by a subordinate, I also can't afford to lose two-thirds of the officers in this detachment."

278

"So, Clay, what was so bad that you decided to resign?" The chief asked.

"Look, I very much appreciate what all three of you are trying to do here, but Karen and I have kicked it around, and both agree it's time for me to retire…if you will let me," Clay explained.

"You certainly deserve to have a long and happy retirement, but I want it to be under the right conditions and under your terms, not like this. If you go now, the perception will be that you were forced out, and for many people, perception is reality," clarified the Chief. "I would like to see you stay on at least through the very end of this case of yours."

Clay started to speak when Aaron interrupted him, "Clay, hear the proposal first."

"Here's what we would like to offer the two of you. I would like to see both of you continue working on this case until you have arrested everyone involved that you possibly can. Both of you will be temporarily supervised by Captain Hamlin during the investigation and will have the full support of SIU. You will work exclusively on the case unless there is a justifiable need for you in the field. Sgt. Dresken will supervise Officer Ramirez, who will be done with training in about two weeks, and will show him around the area," explained Chief Gassett.

The Chief continued, "We are only talking about a few months, and at any time you want, you can pull the plug. Then when the case is done, everyone goes back to their previous positions, and if you still want to retire, I will proudly host your retirement party."

279

Clay sat in silence for a minute before answering, "You have a deal as long as you understand I am going to retire when this is done."

"Understood. One last thing, and I am very serious about this one," the chief explained. "If you ever assault or even threaten to kick the shit out of your supervisor again, there will no longer be a place in this agency for you. Fair enough?"

"Fair," Clay said sheepishly.

Aaron then added, "This is not an order but a suggestion. I think you should talk to Sgt. Dresken and make things right there. I am not suggesting you two become best buds or anything, but you have to be able to be around him without everyone wondering if you are going to tear him in half. You also should know he withdrew his recommended disciplinary letter for you on his own accord. He could have gotten you in serious trouble."

"Thanks, Chief, and you also, Aaron. I appreciate you guys coming all the way over here. I really do," Clay told the men as he stood to shake their hands before they left.

Once the door closed, Clay said simply, "Thanks, kid. You are the best partner and friend I could wish for."

Lisa wrapped Clay in a bear hug and answered, "No problem, Dad. I'm just glad to have you back."

EPILOGUE

Fingerprints lifted from the drone Moe had used for his smuggling scheme came back to Nu Win of Penticton B.C., who Garma identified as one of Moe's nieces. That identification led to the arrest of seven of Moe's relatives in Canada and the seizure of almost $180,000 cash, sixteen kilos of narcotics, forty-four bear gallbladders, and eighty-six pounds of elephant ivory. Through interviews of the Canadian suspects, officers learned that it was in the Penticton home where fentanyl was being added to the heroin the suspects had cut.

By the following January, forty-seven people had been arrested and charged in Washington with drug and wildlife trafficking, along with a myriad of other crimes. Additionally, fourteen more suspects were charged in Canada and eleven in Idaho. In total, the seventy-nine suspects faced over four hundred state and federal felony charges.

Garma and her daughters continued to live in Oroville but were forced to leave their home after losing it and the store. The feds had determined Moe had used the store to launder his illicit income, which gave them grounds to seize the store for government forfeiture. The house was paid for by the same illicit funds. After Garma had written a gut-wrenching letter of apology to Clay and Karen for her husband's actions, she and Karen began talking again. However, both knew there was no way their relationship would ever be the same. Garma got a job as a certified nursing assistant and was working toward getting her full registered nursing credentials.

Sergeant Dresken accepted the position of training sergeant at the headquarters office in Olympia—after his wife filed for divorce and moved with their baby to Spokane to be near her family.

On February 3, 2020, Lisa and Clay were presented with the WDFW Case of the Year Award at their annual in-service training. On that same day, Lisa was awarded the Statewide Officer of the Year Award. While attending that in-service training, Lisa respectfully declined an offer to be promoted to SIU on a permanent basis.

Special Agent Matthew Daniels left the U.S. Fish and Wildlife Service and took a position with U.S. Marshalls—after an internal investigation into his possible embellishment of Clay's culpability in Daniels's warrant affidavit for the search of Clay's home came to an "inconclusive" finding.

Washington Department of Corrections Officer Gregg Meadows was finally terminated two months <u>after</u> reporting to prison to serve out his three-year sentence.

Clay made his retirement official on February 29, 2020, after thirty-one years of service. As promised, Clay's retirement party was hosted by WDFW Chief Jim Gassett.

Captain Aaron Hamlin retired from service only three months after Clay.

Clay, Karen, Lisa, and Emily committed to get together no less than once a month, which they have faithfully kept. Clay and Karen were declared the official dog godparents of Mayhem, who they took care of whenever Lisa and Emily went anywhere overnight.

~ ~ ~ ~ ~ ~ ~ ~ ~ ~ ~ ~ ~ ~ ~ ~ ~

One morning, at his home in the apple orchard he had inherited from his father-in-law, Dennis Swanson was sitting in his leather recliner drinking coffee when an interesting story came on the local news. The story was about a large-scale drug and wildlife smuggling ring busted along the Washington/B.C. border. The story described how an undercover federal agent, working in cooperation with state game wardens, uncovered an international smuggling ring dealing in bear gallbladders, methamphetamines, heroin, fentanyl, and ivory. The "criminal organization" was led by the disgraced former commander of the Myanmar National Police, Moe Omar, who was killed in a shootout with police some months ago. Almost eighty people had since been arrested in Washington, British Columbia, Canada, and Idaho. Officials are still searching for the number two man in the organization, a subject known only as "Mike," who is believed to have fled the country.

Looks like I got out at the perfect time, Dennis Michael Swanson thought to himself with a grin.

ABOUT THE AUTHOR

Todd Vandivert grew up in the Washington D.C. suburbs of northern Virginia until his love of the outdoors led him to the northwest. He attended Washington State University, and in 1978 graduated with a Bachelor of Science degree in Forest Management, hoping to start a career working in the outdoors. While in college he met Judy whom he married just after graduation. A few years later, Todd and Judy had their daughter- Beth.

Todd began his career with the Washington Department of Game in 1979 and has been stationed in three of the six regions of the state. During his career, he started the agency's FTO (Field Training Officer) program and has trained approximately fifty new officers. Todd was the first game warden in the world to design and build a radio-controlled (robotic) deer decoy, now being used in almost every state in the country. He was a Defense Tactics Instructor, as well as a Critical Incident Peer Support Counselor. He has taught classes on ballistic forensics, recognizing false identification, clandestine methamphetamine labs, and wildlife criminal investigations.

Todd served as the editor of the Washington Game Warden Association magazine, the editor of International Game Warden Magazine, and is the author of OPERATION CODY.

He is one of only two officers who have received the WDFW Statewide Officer of the Year award twice. His other awards include; the NWTF Officer of the Year award, the WDFW Case of the Year award, WDFW Detective of the Year award, the Shikar-Safari Club Officer of the Year award, the American Police Hall of Fame award, the Legion of Honor Award, the US Forest Service Award of Merit-Outstanding case, and the NAWEOA (North American Wildlife Enforcement Officers Association)- Outstanding officer award.

Amazon also offers these other books by Detective Todd Vandivert (retired)

Made in the USA
Columbia, SC
11 May 2024